IN LOVE AGAIN

"You have no idea how much pressure I'm under," Todd yelled at Elizabeth. "Everyone expects me to just magically adjust to a whole new life-style. It happens to be pretty tough, Liz, especially with all this grief you keep giving me!"

Elizabeth felt tears spring to her eyes. "Why are you feeling sorry for yourself?" she cried. "Because you have to get used to having your own screening room and a mansion to live in and a brand-new BMW?"

Todd gripped the edge of the table, his knuckles turning white. She had never seen him this angry before. "Cut it out, Liz. Cut it out right now."

"I have to tell you how I feel," she said weakly.

"Well, I'm sick of you judging me," Todd snapped. "You know what? Maybe we should stop seeing each other," he said. "At least till we've figured out what we both want. Since all I seem to do lately is disappoint you."

"Stop seeing each other?" Elizabeth repeated. She felt a queasy sensation in her stomach. This wasn't what she wanted at all. But if Todd wanted to break up with her, she wasn't going to beg him not to. After all, she had her pride. And at the moment it felt as if that was *all* she had.

Bantam Books in the Sweet Valley High Series
Ask your bookseller for the books you have missed

SWEET VALLEY HIGH

IN LOVE AGAIN

Written by
Kate Williams

Created by
FRANCINE PASCAL

BANTAM BOOKS
NEW YORK · TORONTO · LONDON · SYDNEY · AUCKLAND

RL 6, IL age 12 and up

IN LOVE AGAIN
A Bantam Book / October 1989

Sweet Valley High is a registered trademark of Francine Pascal.

Conceived by Francine Pascal

*Produced by Daniel Weiss Associates, Inc., 27 West 20th Street,
New York, NY 10011*

Cover art by James Mathewuse

ISBN 0-553-28193-3

Published simultaneously in the United States and Canada

*Bantam Books are published by Bantam Books, a division of
Bantam Doubleday Dell Publishing Group, Inc. Its trademark,
consisting of the words "Bantam Books" and the portrayal of a
rooster, is Registered in U.S. Patent and Trademark Office and in
other countries. Marca Registrada. Bantam Books, 666 Fifth
Avenue, New York, New York 10103.*

PRINTED IN THE UNITED STATES OF AMERICA

OPM   0 9 8 7 6 5 4 3 2 1

IN LOVE AGAIN

One

"I don't believe it," Lila Fowler said incredulously. She put down her fork, her eyes sparkling as Jessica Wakefield filled her in on the news that was spreading like wildfire through Sweet Valley High. "Are you saying that Elizabeth and Todd really got back together over the weekend? And that she broke up with Jeffrey French?"

"It's like something out of a movie," Amy Sutton said, sighing dramatically. "It sounds *so* romantic."

"You're not kidding," Cara Walker agreed.

"So give us all the details," Lila urged Jessica.

Jessica raised one eyebrow and regarded her friends. "Haven't you guys heard enough?" she demanded.

"No!" the three girls screamed in unison.

Jessica grinned. Secretly she was enjoying the attention. There was nothing Jessica liked better than being in the middle of the action. And right now she was more than in the middle of it—she was its twin!

"I didn't think Liz and Todd would get back together," Amy said, gazing across the cafeteria at Elizabeth, who was eating lunch several tables away with her best friend, Enid Rollins. "I mean, here she was, totally involved with Jeffrey and everything."

"But she and Todd had *history*," Cara said knowingly.

Jessica shook her head. "I knew the second we found out Todd was moving back to Sweet Valley that Jeffrey didn't stand a chance."

The three girls thought this over for a minute in silence. The fact was, everyone at Sweet Valley High had been following Elizabeth Wakefield's love life with fascination ever since her old boyfriend had moved back to town a few weeks ago. Elizabeth and Todd Wilkins had been a steady item for a long time, and then his father had been transferred to Burlington, Vermont. They had tried to keep the relationship going for a while, but the distance had proved insurmountable. Although they remained friends, they both began dating other people.

Then Elizabeth had fallen in love with Jeffrey French, and she and Todd gradually lost touch.

"And I thought she and Jeffrey were so happy together," Lila observed. She leaned over to steal a french fry off Amy's plate. Lila Fowler never forgot a grudge, and the fact that she herself had made a play for Jeffrey when he first moved to town hadn't exactly endeared her to either Elizabeth or Jeffrey. As a matter of fact, she had tried to come between them several times.

"But Todd's much cuter," Amy commented. "I think Liz did the right thing."

Jessica gave Amy a dirty look. "Liz didn't go back to Todd because she thinks he's *cuter*, Ame. The fact is, they're really in love." She shook her head, despairing at her friend's lack of insight. "Besides, now that Todd's father is president of Varitronics—now that he's practically a millionaire . . ." She let her voice drop off knowingly. "Why shouldn't Liz do what anyone with half a brain would?" She popped a french fry into her mouth, then smiled. "You can just tell she did the right thing, every time you see them together."

"Who gets to see them together?" Amy pointed out. "Now that Todd's a Lovett Academy student, nobody sees him at all!"

Amy had a point. Todd's father had returned to Sweet Valley to take over as president of Varitronics, the computer firm for which he worked. And the new job came with a whole new life-style, which included a luxurious new house and a new private school for Todd.

"I don't see why he wanted to go to Lovett Academy, anyway," Amy grumbled. "I guess he doesn't think Sweet Valley High is good enough for him anymore, now that his dad's a hotshot corporate president."

"Oh, please," Lila said, giving Amy an imperious smile. "Everyone knows Lovett Academy is the most prestigious private school in the whole state! It's only natural Todd's parents would want him to go there now that they've become such important people." Lila considered herself an expert on Lovett. Not only did she know some Lovett students through the Sweet Valley Country Club, but also, as one of Sweet Valley High's richest students, she considered herself the expert on anything exclusive— and costly.

"So, how come *you* don't go to Lovett, Lila?" Amy demanded.

Lila shrugged. "Daddy thinks it's important for me to learn about the real world."

Amy stifled a giggle. Lila had a monthly

allowance that was bigger than some students' yearly allowances. She wasn't exactly someone who went out of her way to meet people from different backgrounds! The thought of her going to public school to learn about the real world struck both Amy and Jessica as pretty funny.

"Look," Lila said, sounding annoyed, "I don't see why you're all so critical of Todd for wanting the very best. I happen to know some terrific people who go to Lovett. That school has the best sports facilities, great teachers, small classes—"

"And the biggest bank accounts!" Cara interrupted, giggling.

"You know," Jessica said, grinning at Amy, "I think I may have learned too *much* about the real world lately. Don't you think it would be good for someone like me to spend a year at Lovett?"

Amy groaned. "Just what we need—Jessica Stuck-Up Wakefield."

"I'm serious," Jessica protested. "I think Lovett Academy might have a lot to offer me. Todd told Liz that they get to take Russian and Chinese there, not just boring old French and Spanish."

"Good reason to go, Jess," Lila said sarcastically. "Especially since you're such a world traveler."

Amy narrowed her eyes at Jessica. "I don't suppose your new interest in Lovett has anything to do with the fact that you think you failed your math test this morning, does it? And that Skip Harmon ignored you in the lunch line?"

Jessica shook her head. "Don't be ridiculous," she said. She wasn't about to tell her friends that she didn't like being out of the limelight, but that was exactly the way she had felt ever since Todd moved back to town.

Jessica wasn't used to having her twin's life be more exciting than her own. In fact, far from it. But lately Jessica felt that things had seemed just a tiny bit stale at Sweet Valley High. She wanted intrigue, and she was prepared to do whatever was necessary to get it. If that meant transferring to a new school, she was ready and willing!

"Lovett has so many advantages," Jessica continued. "Just think about all the new people I could meet there."

"When Jessica says people," Amy said, grinning, "you know she really means guys!"

Jessica shrugged. "I admit it. When Todd took Liz and me on a tour of Lovett, I saw more cute guys in a day than you'd see around this place in a year. More cute, *rich* guys," she added.

"Maybe this isn't the time to remind you what happened to that one cute rich boy you met from Lovett," Lila added.

Jessica turned scarlet. It was true. Sheffield Eastman, a Lovett Academy junior, had turned out to be a major disappointment. Jessica had met him through Todd, and she had set her heart on becoming Sheffield's girlfriend. He looked like a young version of Paul Newman, and he had the bank account and the glamour to go along with his good looks! How was she supposed to have known that all Sheffield cared about was dedicating himself to charity work—and that he wanted to spend his senior year working and living in a shelter for the homeless?

"Just because Sheffield bombed out doesn't mean there aren't plenty of other guys at Lovett," Jessica told Lila. "I saw enough during my one visit to be sure of that."

"Maybe we should all go there," Amy said quickly.

Lila groaned. "I think you're nuts, Jess. The Lovett admissions exams are very hard. You know that Todd had to take special exams in science, languages, and literature. You won't be doing anything but studying if you want to get in. Especially," she added condescendingly, "since your father isn't a brand-new company president like Todd's."

"I still think it's worth looking into," Jessica said. She got to her feet and picked up her tray. "I'm going to get rid of this disgusting chicken salad, then go over to see how my sister's love life is doing." She giggled. "Besides, maybe Liz has heard more about Lovett from Todd." Her eyes sparkled. "There's still a lot I want to find out about private school before I rule it out completely!"

"Here comes trouble," Enid Rollins said under her breath. "Trouble with a capital T, and that stands for Twin."

Elizabeth giggled. She and Enid had been close friends for so long that they could practically read each other's minds. Elizabeth had been pouring her heart out to Enid, telling her all about Todd, and Enid had guessed that the last thing she wanted right then was to be interrupted by her sister.

"Liz!" Jessica cried, sliding into a vacant chair at the table. "Mind if I join you guys?" she asked, helping herself to one of the chocolate-chip cookies Elizabeth had on her tray.

Elizabeth smiled at her twin. As far as their looks went, the two girls were absolutely identical. Blond, slender, and unusually pretty, they both had sparkling blue-green eyes and tiny dimples that showed when they smiled. They each had perfect size-six figures and could swap clothes easily. No one but their family and closest friends could tell them apart.

But the twins had personalities as opposite as their looks were similar. Jessica was four minutes younger than her sister, and she liked to claim that was what made her so carefree. *Carefree* wasn't always the word Elizabeth would have used to describe her sister. *Careless* was sometimes more like it. Jessica moved through activities, loyalties, and romances with lightning speed. She talked fast, dressed in all the latest styles, and was constantly looking for ways to make life more colorful and exciting.

Elizabeth liked life at a slower pace. She had a few extra-special friends, not big crowds of them like Jessica, although she was one of the most popular students at Sweet Valley High. She loved reading and studying and dreamed of becoming a writer one day, a dream she was helping to realize by working on *The Oracle*, the school newspaper. Elizabeth didn't mind being the responsible half of the Wakefield twins. But every once in a while she wished Jessica were just a tiny bit calmer and more dependable.

"I've come over here on a mission," Jessica announced, clasping her hands together. "Tell me everything you possibly can about Lovett Academy."

Elizabeth laughed and glanced at Enid. "You must have ESP, Jess. We were just talking about Lovett."

"I think it may be the right place for me," Jessica declared. "Todd likes it, right? Doesn't he think he's getting all sorts of things there that he couldn't possibly get here at Sweet Valley?"

"There's more he *isn't* getting," Enid said. "For instance, time with Elizabeth."

Elizabeth sighed. "True," she said. "It seems strange to have Todd back in town but not here at school." She looked at her twin with an amused smile. "I hope you're kidding about Lovett. You'd hate it there, Jess. It's snobby, and they have to do about ten times as much homework as we do."

Jessica sat up straighter. "You might not be aware of this, Liz, but I happen to be very interested in that sort of thing."

"What sort of thing? Snobbishness? More homework?" Elizabeth asked.

"You really don't seem like the Lovett type," Enid remarked. "Would you be able to stand dressing so formally every day? They wouldn't let you wear miniskirts and wild clothes there."

"They didn't look that formal the day we visited," Jessica said doubtfully.

Elizabeth shrugged. "Well, they have a pretty strict dress code, except on Fridays, when they can wear whatever they want, as long as it isn't jeans. And the students I've seen tend to dress much more formally and more conservatively than you do. Enid has a point, Jess."

"Still," Jessica said, "think of all the interesting people I'd meet."

Elizabeth glanced meaningfully at Enid. "Interesting *boys*," she said.

Jessica jumped to her feet. "Thanks for taking me so seriously, Liz," she said in a hurt voice. "If you don't feel like telling me more about Lovett, I'll just have to find out more about it myself!"

And with that she stormed off, leaving Elizabeth and Enid staring after her.

That afternoon Elizabeth just couldn't seem to keep her mind on the poem Mr. Collins was discussing during English class. All she could think about was Todd and how lucky they were to be back together.

Ever since Todd had moved back to Sweet Valley, she felt as though her life had been knocked off-balance. It was the biggest shock Elizabeth had ever experienced. One day everything had been calm, settled, routine. Then she heard that Todd was returning and suddenly everything changed.

She honestly hadn't known how she was going to feel until Todd actually arrived. Before that, she and Jeffrey had tried to deal with things as rationally as they could. It wasn't as though Elizabeth had known from the start that her relationship with Jeffrey would fall apart just because Todd was coming back. In fact, she had been amazed by the strength of her feelings for Todd. She had been prepared to experience some pangs of nostalgia, but not such an overwhelmingly strong sensation of love.

The hardest thing had been hurting Jeffrey. Jeffrey French was one of the kindest, best-natured boys Elizabeth had ever known. He had been a real friend to Elizabeth, as well as a boyfriend. In fact, his behavior for the past few weeks—since Todd had moved back from Vermont—had been so selfless that tears came to

Elizabeth's eyes every time she thought about it.

Jeffrey could easily have conspired to keep Elizabeth and Todd apart, especially since Courtney Kane, the daughter of the CEO of Varitronics and Todd's classmate at Lovett Academy, had been determined to make Todd her boyfriend. Because of Courtney, Elizabeth and Todd's relationship had almost been destroyed. But Jeffrey had actually intervened on their behalf. As he told Elizabeth in a tearful meeting later, he had to be sure she really wanted to be with him, and not Todd.

But what he learned was that it wasn't all over between Elizabeth and Todd. Far from it, in fact.

Enid had asked Elizabeth at lunch earlier whether it was strange getting back together with Todd after such a long time. Thinking about it now, Elizabeth had to admit that Todd sometimes seemed like someone other than the boy she used to date. He had a new house, a new car, and more money to spend. But surely those things weren't very important. What *was* important was that when they were together, she experienced all the old feelings of affection for him, only stronger. He was so funny, so kind, so clever. Just thinking about the warmth of his lips on hers when they kissed gave her a tingling feeling.

Suddenly the bell rang, and her classmates started gathering their notebooks. She had to shake herself out of her reverie.

This is ridiculous, she chided herself, getting to her feet and rummaging around for her books. She felt as though everyone could tell what she was thinking.

"Liz," Cara Walker said, turning to her and smiling, "why are you in such a daze?"

Elizabeth blushed. She had a feeling it was going to take some time before she got used to being madly in love again.

Two

After school Jessica was waiting for Elizabeth outside by the Fiat Spider the two girls shared.

"Could you drop me off downtown?" Jessica asked her twin. "I need to go to the library to look up some stuff on Lovett."

Elizabeth narrowed her eyes at Jessica. "You're not really serious about this stuff, are you? Jess, you're the last person in the world I can imagine at that place. I told you what it's like."

"If Todd's happy there, why won't I be?" Jessica said stubbornly.

"To tell you the truth, I'm not sure Lovett is the right school for Todd, either." Elizabeth didn't like to prejudge anyone, but several of the Lovett Academy students, especially Courtney

Kane, had been very snooty and unkind to Elizabeth. "I just wonder if Todd's not too down-to-earth for a place like Lovett."

"You're not just saying that because you miss him and want him at Sweet Valley High all day?" Jessica asked.

Elizabeth laughed. "You may have a point," she admitted as she hopped into the driver's seat.

"So listen," Jessica said eagerly after they headed out of the school parking lot. "Is it really as wonderful being back with Todd as you thought? Is it totally romantic?"

"Yes," Elizabeth said, smiling softly.

"Poor Jeffrey," Jessica said, settling back in the passenger seat and unwrapping a stick of gum. "He looks totally devastated. I saw him moping around his locker today looking so depressed, I didn't think he'd have the strength to pick up his books."

A deep frown creased Elizabeth's forehead. "Jeffrey will be all right," she mumbled. The truth was, Jeffrey's undisguised sadness was the only shadow crossing Elizabeth's happiness. And, uncharacteristically, she was trying to ignore it. She just didn't know what else to do.

"I wonder if he'll pine away. Do you think he'll do something drastic?" Jessica asked.

"Of course not," Elizabeth said. "He's way too sensible. And he's too nice and too good-looking to be alone for long. He'll probably forget about me before you know it." She couldn't help feeling a pang as she said that. Although she was sure of her love for Todd, she still cared about Jeffrey.

"Ha!" Jessica exclaimed. "I don't think Jeffrey's ever going to forget about you, Liz."

The girls were quiet as Elizabeth maneuvered in and out of traffic. "Anyway," Jessica said cheerfully, snapping her gum, "I think you did the right thing. I like Jeffrey and everything, but he's a little on the bland side. Whereas Todd is fantastic. And now—well, he has everything now. Absolutely everything."

Elizabeth frowned. "Here's the library," she said shortly, pulling the Fiat over to the curb to let Jessica hop out.

"See you tonight!" Jessica said gaily. And before Elizabeth could say another word, Jessica sprinted up the steps and into the town library.

That night the Wakefields barbecued their dinner outdoors, taking advantage of the balmy California weather.

17

"I wish Steve were here. He loves grilled steaks," Alice Wakefield said. Steven, the twins' eighteen-year-old brother, was a freshman at the nearby state university. He came home occasionally for weekends or vacations, but his schedule had been so busy lately that he hadn't had time to come home.

"Alice," Ned Wakefield said with an appreciative smile, "how is it you manage to put together a meal like this after a ten-hour workday?"

Mrs. Wakefield worked full-time as an interior designer, and Mr. Wakefield was an attorney. Often, both had to work long hours.

Mrs. Wakefield smiled at her daughters. "Call it a little daughterly assistance," she said, smoothing back her blond hair.

Elizabeth waited for Jessica to admit that she hadn't helped with dinner one bit, since she had been at the library until about half an hour ago. But Jessica didn't volunteer that information. She simply beamed while Mr. Wakefield praised the girls for helping their mother.

In fact, Jessica seemed to take her father's praise as her cue to begin her Lovett Academy campaign speech.

"Speaking of long hours and hard work," she

18

said, pausing for effect, "I've been giving a great deal of thought lately to the kind of education I'm receiving at Sweet Valley High."

Mr. and Mrs. Wakefield exchanged amused glances. "Do you mean the new cheers you're learning at cheerleading practice? Or the new handshake at the sorority?" her father asked.

"I'm serious," Jessica insisted. "A young mind needs an opportunity to expand its intellectual horizons."

Elizabeth had to stifle a giggle. It was obvious that Jessica had spent the afternoon memorizing Lovett's catalog.

"What exactly are you trying to say, Jessica?" Mrs. Wakefield asked.

"I just think I'm the kind of student who needs a private school," Jessica declared. "I need all the benefits of small classes, extra attention from teachers, exclusive teaching methods—"

"Enormous tuition bills," Mr. Wakefield added dryly.

Jessica looked outraged. "Daddy! Don't you want me to have the finest education money can buy?"

"Jessica, I'm a little surprised by this," Mrs. Wakefield observed. "You know that you were always welcome to explore the option of private school. Don't you remember telling us that you'd rather die than leave your friends? That there was more to education than just books? That things like cheerleading meant the world to you?"

Jessica made a face. "That was ages ago. I'm much more mature now. I realize how important it is to be in the—" She paused, obviously trying to remember one of the phrases from the catalog. "In the right learning atmosphere!" she exclaimed.

"Remember when Liz was interested in that boarding school in Switzerland, the one with the creative writing program?" Mrs. Wakefield went on. "Weren't you the one who campaigned hardest to get her to stay at Sweet Valley High, where you said she belonged?"

"Oh," Jessica said, shrugging. "Well, Switzerland's a little extreme. I was thinking of someplace local."

"Local?" Elizabeth asked with feigned innocence. "What about Lovett Academy?"

Jessica's face lit up. "Exactly!" she cried. "Mom, Dad, I'm absolutely sure Lovett's the place for me. Think of how refined I'd get. Hanging out with those kids from the country club, learning how to speak Russian and play polo. It's bound to help me get into a better college," she added hastily when she saw the expression on her father's face at the mention of polo.

Mr. Wakefield raised his eyebrows. "Have you done any research on this, or is it just an idea right now?"

Jessica looked hurt. "Would I bother you and Mom about something so important without taking the time to look into it first?" No one answered this question, so Jessica quickly filled her parents in on some of the details about Lovett she had learned at the library.

"Well," Mr. Wakefield began when Jessica had finished explaining, "your mother and I have never felt strongly one way or the other on this issue. We really felt it was up to you girls. If you're serious about Lovett, Jessica, why don't you try to find out more about it? I don't see what harm it could do."

Jessica grinned. As far as she was concerned, she was as good as admitted to Lovett already! It would only be a matter of time before she would be hanging out at the exclusive private school, meeting fabulous people and starting a whole new life.

Even though she had been to Todd's house a few times, Elizabeth still couldn't get used to parking the Fiat at the top of the Wilkinses' huge driveway and ringing the bell at the massive front doors of their new mansion. The Wilkinses' old home had been very similar to the Wakefields'—a comfortable split-level house in a pretty part of Sweet Valley. Their new home was entirely different; it was more like a mansion. In fact, *home* was probably the wrong word to describe the huge place, with its high ceilings, marble floors, elaborate furnishings, ballroom, and Olympic-size pool!

As Elizabeth waited for Todd to answer the door, she nervously shifted her weight from one foot to the other. She had mixed feelings about the Wilkinses' sudden shift in social status. The raise and powerful position Todd's father had been given meant a new life-style for the whole family. There were parties given by wealthy people in and around town that Todd's father was invited to, parties where Todd was expected to make an appearance. Then there was the question of school. All the children of Varitronics' senior management went to Lovett— it was expected, too. They all had big allowances and fancy cars, and they went into Los Angeles on weekends to hang around in Westwood.

So far, Elizabeth had been so ecstatic to be back with Todd that she hadn't really stopped to think how these new changes would affect him. But that evening, thinking back over Jessica's conversation with her parents, she wondered if Todd had started to like Lovett better than Sweet Valley High. Could she fit in with his new life? Or would she continue to feel out of place? Then Todd opened the door, and Elizabeth immediately forgot all her misgivings.

"Hi," he said, his eyes crinkling up in a warm smile.

One look at Todd and Elizabeth's heart melted. His brown curly hair, his beautiful eyes, his strong jaw . . . he was so handsome. "I've missed you," he said, embracing her warmly.

Elizabeth felt her heart begin to pound. "I missed you, too. Is that crazy? Just after one day?"

"We have a lot of time to catch up on," Todd said. He took her hand and led her through the imposing front hall of the new house to the ornate living room.

"I brought over some homework," Elizabeth said, somewhat apologetically, "and a few things I told Penny Ayala I'd try to have finished by tomorrow for *The Oracle*. . . ."

Todd looked upset. "Oh, no. You have work to do? I was hoping we could watch the movie

Dad videotaped last night. I haven't even used the screening room yet."

Elizabeth laughed. "That's right. I forgot about the screening room." There was a small room off the living room with a movie screen that covered the back wall, and a stereo, a video player, and a movie projector. "I guess my homework can wait," Elizabeth said. She giggled as Todd pretended to twist her arm. "OK, OK! I give in! Let's watch a movie!"

Ten minutes later the two of them were curled up on the soft couch in the screening room, watching the movie that Mr. Wilkins had taped for them. Elizabeth couldn't believe how good it felt sitting there with Todd's arm around her. It was as if they had rolled back time, as if Todd had never moved and there were only the two of them. If it weren't for the glamorous new surroundings, she could almost believe they were back in the Wilkinses' old living room, watching TV.

"It's so good being here with you, Liz," Todd said when the movie had ended. "I can't believe how lucky I am. Sometimes I have to pinch myself to prove I'm not dreaming."

"I know how you feel," Elizabeth said softly. "I didn't think people ever got second chances. Todd, when you moved, I was miserable. I missed you so much! I never in a million years thought you'd come back."

Todd kissed her, and Elizabeth felt her heart begin to pound.

"Let's spend every minute together that we can," Todd said, hugging her even closer to him. "I hate having to be apart all day long. Let's make sure we spend as many afternoons and evenings together as possible." His eyes were bright with emotion. "I feel like we need to get to know each other all over again. We have so much to talk about. How about a trip to Secca Lake tomorrow right after school?"

Elizabeth didn't answer. She had an *Oracle* meeting the next afternoon. Penny wanted to talk to the entire staff about some of the problems she had noticed in the way the paper was written and produced.

But the look on Todd's face was so intense that she couldn't imagine saying no. Secca Lake was one of their special places. Maybe she could miss the meeting, just this once. Would Penny really be that upset if she wasn't there?

"I'd love to go to the lake with you," she said. "The only thing is, I promised Penny I'd go to this *Oracle* meeting after school. I think it's going to be pretty important."

Todd shook his head. "Don't tell me I'm

25

going to have to wait until tomorrow night to see you! I won't be able to stand it!"

Elizabeth started to giggle. She couldn't resist the desperate look on his face. "Well, then, how about picking me up at school at four o'clock? I know it'll take you about an hour to drive back from Lovett. And that way I can put in an appearance at the meeting and still get to see you," she suggested.

She knew deep down that she really shouldn't plan to leave the meeting early. But she just couldn't help herself. Todd was all that mattered to her now. And she was just as determined as Todd was to spend every free minute together, even if it meant cutting back on her activities!

Three

Elizabeth glanced nervously at her watch. It was Tuesday afternoon at three-thirty, and she was supposed to meet Todd in half an hour. She hoped that Penny would quickly run through the things she wanted to talk about at the *Oracle* meeting.

She hurried down the hallway and opened the door to the office just as Jeffrey came around the corner. She had forgotten that Jeffrey would be at the meeting, but it made sense—he was a photographer for the paper, after all. Why hadn't she realized he would be there?

Elizabeth had barely spoken to Jeffrey since the night of Todd's party. She said hello to him when they passed each other in the hallway at school, and that was all. In fact, she had a feeling that Jeffrey was going out of his way to avoid her. Not that she blamed him. If he had left *her* for an old girlfriend, Elizabeth was sure she would have reacted the same way.

She felt strange about seeing him, too. Right now, for instance, she didn't have the faintest idea what to say. She just stared at him, feeling a blush spread across her face.

"Hi," Jeffrey said. His expression was serious.

"Hi. How are you?" Elizabeth asked.

Jeffrey was about to respond when Penny raced up to them. "Oh, good. You guys are here. We have a ton of stuff to get through. Come on in, and let's get started."

Elizabeth glanced at Jeffrey, wondering if he was as grateful for the interruption as she was.

Inside the office, Olivia Davidson was hard at work on the layout for that week's paper. "Hi, guys," she said, waving at them when they walked into the room. She gave Elizabeth a sympathetic smile. "Poor Liz. You really got pounded on today in math class."

Elizabeth cleared her throat. "Oh, it was nothing," she said, hoping Jeffrey hadn't been paying attention. But when she glanced his way, she saw that he was staring at her with surprise. It wasn't like Elizabeth to get into trouble at school.

"It figures," Olivia went on. "The one time

you don't have your homework done, you get called on first. Isn't that the way it always goes?" Olivia shook her head, her brown, frizzy hair tumbling around her face. She was the arts editor for *The Oracle*, and a good friend of Elizabeth's.

Elizabeth wished Olivia hadn't chosen that moment to discuss the way she'd gotten caught unprepared in math class. The fact was, Elizabeth always did her homework diligently. And if it hadn't been for the night before with Todd...

Jeffrey kept staring at her, his green eyes penetrating. Did he guess what was going on? Elizabeth wondered. Was he secretly thinking, *You weren't like this when you and I were going out*?

"Let's get started," Penny said briskly. "Mr. Collins has made a list of problems he's noticed with the paper, and some ideas he has, as well. The real point of this meeting is to get feedback from all of you so we can figure out how to make the paper better."

As she took a seat by the window, Elizabeth could barely take her eyes off the clock near the door. There were only twenty minutes left until Todd would be meeting her outside. If only they had said four-thirty! Or if only there was some way she could get in touch with him and tell him not to come! She couldn't bear the interrupting the meeting to leave early—especially with Jeffrey there, watching her every move!

Penny started the meeting by listing some ideas she had received from people about revising the layout of the front page using graphics. Rod Sullivan, a junior, who had just begun dating arts editor Olivia Davidson, had submitted some particularly good ideas. Then Penny discussed the school's reaction to the cartoon strip the paper had been running. She suggested adding an advice column to *The Oracle*, and everyone agreed that was a good idea. Then it was time to talk about the "Eyes and Ears" column, the gossip page Elizabeth had written and edited for a long time.

"I'm not sure," Penny said, chewing the eraser on the end of her pencil, "but I think it may be time to scrap 'Eyes and Ears' and try something new. What do you think, Liz?"

Elizabeth shifted in her chair. It was ten minutes to four. There was no way the meeting would be over in time for her to escape without embarrassment. "Actually," she said, taking a deep breath, "I like the idea of starting a new project. But I have to admit I won't be able to go into much detail now. I have to meet someone at four o'clock. Is there any way I can write up my ideas tonight and get them to you tomorrow?"

"Fine," Penny said. But the look on her face said it wasn't fine at all. It was clear that she was disappointed in Elizabeth.

Elizabeth didn't blame Penny for being angry. She knew it was wrong to leave such an important editorial meeting. But the thought of seeing Todd again made everything bearable—even the disapproving look on Jeffrey's face when she slid out of her chair at four o'clock.

"What do you think you're doing?" Amy Sutton demanded, coming up behind Jessica in the school library. "You and I were supposed to go over the new cheerleading routine in the gym this afternoon. It *is* Tuesday, remember?"

"Mmm," Jessica muttered, her pen between her teeth. "Listen, Ame, I'm really busy right now. I can't talk."

Amy ignored her and pulled up a chair. "Busy with what?" She narrowed her eyes when she saw the Lovett Academy catalog. "What's that? Jess, don't tell me you're really serious about this private school stuff!"

Jessica scrutinized the first page of the catalog. "Admissions," she read out loud. "Every candidate must take at least three out of five of

Lovett's entrance exams in the following subjects: languages, literature, math, science..."

Amy twisted a lock of blond hair around one finger. "I can't believe this. It's one thing to joke about transferring to Lovett, but it's another to start wasting your free periods looking up stuff about admissions!"

"Rats," Jessica said, setting the catalog aside. "Looks like I'll have to take some admissions tests. But how hard can they be?" she added a moment later, her face brightening. "They probably just want to know who your favorite polo player is and when you're planning your next trip to Europe."

"I think you should cut this out," Amy advised Jessica. "Those kids are really stuck up. You know they must be bad if *Lila* says they are!"

Jessica shrugged. "I know what's best for me, Amy. And right now I know I really need to switch to Lovett." Frowning, she looked around the library. "This just isn't the right sort of atmosphere for me. Take my word for it, Amy, Lovett is."

"So, are you going to waste the next few months studying for some really grueling entrance exams?" Amy asked.

Jessica shook her head. "No way! Look, the

next test date is two weeks from Saturday." She grinned. "How tough can it be? I'll just brush up on a couple of things, buy a new outfit for my interview, and before you know it, I'll be a Lovett Academy girl."

When Amy looked doubtful, Jessica added, "And I'll get to know zillions of cute guys to introduce you to. Come on, Amy. It isn't just me I'm thinking of!"

"Private school," Amy muttered. Then she got up. "I'm going to see if Maria wants to work on this routine with me. No point in waiting around for you anymore. Now that you're going to be a Lovett Academy girl, I guess you won't have time for stupid things like cheerleading!" Amy turned and stomped off toward the exit.

Jessica stuck out her tongue at Amy's back. Small-minded people like Amy Sutton were exactly what she needed to get away from!

"Hi, gorgeous," Todd said. He gave Elizabeth a sweet, lingering kiss. "Do you have any idea how wonderful it is to see you?"

Elizabeth felt her spirits lifting. Hard as it had been to tear herself away from the *Oracle* meeting, she was sure now that she had done the right thing. After all, she rationalized, this was

33

a very important time for her and Todd. They needed to be together more often to reestablish their relationship. Their feelings for each other were very strong, but everything still was so new and tentative. Besides, they had to overcome the problem of being at different schools.

"Tell me everything that happened to you today," Elizabeth said, climbing into the passenger seat of Todd's new BMW.

Todd laughed. "It was a typical day at Lovett. We had junior seminars first thing this morning. Then a special interdisciplinary course on ancient Greece. All that was great. But lunch hour!" He rolled his eyes. "Some of these kids are really amazing. Today Tim Sollers told us that he's been invited to dinner at Michael Jackson's house. So then a whole bunch of kids started competing, dropping names—you know." He shrugged. "Some of the kids are nice, but some of them are hard to be around. I really miss Sweet Valley High."

"Have you talked to your parents about it?" Elizabeth asked.

For the rest of the ride to Secca Lake, they discussed the advantages and the disadvantages of Lovett. Todd believed that it was really important to his father that he stay enrolled in the school where his colleagues' children were.

"Every time we go somewhere—like to something at the Sweet Valley Country Club—everyone talks about Lovett. I think Dad would be really upset if I asked to go back to Sweet Valley High."

Elizabeth was silent. She didn't like to think that Todd would make such an important decision just because he thought his father wanted it. But she sympathized with his position nonetheless.

"And besides, I guess Lovett isn't all that bad," Todd went on. "I met a guy I like a lot—Sandy Winters. He likes soccer and basketball, just like I do. And Sheffield Eastman is a really nice guy. Not many people from a family as privileged as his would consider giving it all up to live with the homeless."

Elizabeth had to hide a smile, remembering her twin sister's reaction to Sheffield's philanthropy. "I'm sure there are nice kids there," she said quietly. "And knowing you, you'll find the really great ones to be friends with."

Todd didn't say anything, and Elizabeth couldn't help wondering if her optimism was justified. She had met several of the students at Lovett, and they really did seem to have different values. Would Todd be happy there? Was it really the best place for him?

But by the time they reached the lake, all her worries were forgotten. They went straight to their favorite place, a grassy bank rolling down to the clear blue water. Todd spread out a blanket, and they lay down on their backs, holding hands and staring up at the sky.

"What a perfect place. What a perfect day," Todd whispered, squeezing her hand.

Elizabeth shivered. "Can't you almost feel the earth spinning underneath us?" she whispered back.

When Todd propped himself up on one elbow to look tenderly down at her, she thought her heart would burst from happiness. "You know," he said softly, tracing her jaw with his finger, "you make me feel so good, Elizabeth Wakefield. Do you have any idea how good?"

Todd's finger tickled a little, and Elizabeth giggled. "No, I don't," she teased him. "How good?"

A shadow crossed Todd's face for just a second. "So good that I forgot all about the fact that I had basketball practice this afternoon. Coach Robinson wasn't too happy when he saw me leaving." He grinned. "But there'll be plenty of days for basketball practice. How many chances do I get to lie here with you on such a beautiful afternoon?"

Elizabeth frowned. "You really missed practice?" she asked.

"Yep," Todd said. "I couldn't wait to see you. I didn't exactly mind missing practice for you, either." He grinned at her.

Elizabeth believed Todd when he said that he didn't mind breaking a commitment to spend time with her. Right now she didn't care much about leaving the *Oracle* meeting early, either.

But sooner or later she and Todd were going to have to make changes. They couldn't keep disappointing people who relied on them, even if it meant spending less time together.

Elizabeth couldn't imagine doing that now, though, especially when Todd pulled her into his arms and kissed her.

Four

The rest of the week flew by for Elizabeth as she tried to juggle school, meetings, friends—and Todd. By Friday afternoon she definitely felt ready for a weekend.

"Elizabeth!" Penny called, catching her on the way to the *Oracle* office, her arms filled with books.

"Hi," Elizabeth said, turning and smiling. "I was just going to work on my column."

Penny frowned. "That's what I wanted to talk to you about. Do you have time to sit down for a minute?"

Usually Penny was sunny and good-natured, but just then her expression was grim. "Sure," Elizabeth said, following Penny into the office and closing the door behind her. "Did you read the ideas I gave you of possible replacement columns for 'Eyes and Ears'?"

"Yes, Liz. But that's not what's on my mind." She was pacing back and forth, as if she were trying to summon her courage. "This is the hardest thing in the world to say to you, of all people. You've always been one of the hardest-working staff members on the newspaper. But during the past week or so, I don't know..." She shrugged. "Did you forget to proofread your column this week? It went to the printer with four typos in it." She handed Elizabeth a copy of the paper. "This just isn't like you, Liz."

Elizabeth stared down at the incriminating typos, appalled. "Oh, no!" she cried. "I can't believe I missed these!"

"Tell me the truth," Penny said after a minute. "Are you starting to feel that you have too many other commitments to manage the column?"

Elizabeth shook her head vehemently. "Absolutely not, Penny. I don't know what got into me, but I can guarantee you it won't happen again."

"I wouldn't have even brought it up," Penny said slowly, "but you left the meeting early the other day, and then I haven't seen you in here much. You've been so preoccupied..."

She paused, but Penny didn't have to complete the sentence for Elizabeth to know what she meant. *You've been so busy with Todd.*

Elizabeth was ashamed of herself. She had been negligent and irresponsible. She had no business leaving that meeting early, and she certainly shouldn't have let typos in her column slide past her. One of the things the newspaper staff prided itself on was maintaining a high standard of accuracy, and now Elizabeth had made them all look sloppy because of her carelessness. "Please accept my apology," she said to Penny. "I won't let it happen again."

Penny smiled warmly at her. "OK. I believe you. Let's drop it, then."

But Elizabeth couldn't just forget it like that. She felt strangely depressed for the rest of the day. And when she met Todd after school that day at the Box Tree Café, she immediately brought up the conversation with Penny.

"Listen, something happened today," she said, just as Todd said, "Liz, we have to talk about something."

They both stared at each other, then laughed uneasily.

"You first," Elizabeth told him.

"OK." Todd took a deep breath. "The coach

told me today that if I miss one more practice I'm off the team."

Elizabeth stared at him. "How many have you missed?" she asked.

"Three. Once was a mistake—I didn't know about it because Coach changed the time. The other two times, though, I just wanted to see you more than I wanted to work out with the rest of the guys." Todd looked miserable. "I still feel that way. But I do want to play for the team. It's one of the best things about being at Lovett. And I don't want to get in trouble there, either. My parents would be pretty mad at me if I messed up such a great opportunity," he added.

"Well, it turns out we may be having the same problem," Elizabeth said, putting her hand over his on the table. She relayed the conversation she'd had with Penny that afternoon. "Maybe spending time together everyday after school isn't such a great idea," she concluded.

Todd nodded slowly. "I don't want you to get in trouble with the newspaper. You love writing, and it would be terrible not to keep up with it after all you've done so far."

"I know," Elizabeth said. "But we can still see each other in the evenings, even if we both have stuff to do after school."

"Right," Todd said cheerfully. "And on weekends, too. There's plenty of time."

Elizabeth smiled, but she knew deep down that seeing each other on weekday evenings wasn't going to be all that easy. They would both have a lot of homework to do.

"This might sound stupid," Elizabeth said softly, "but sometimes, during the day at school, it feels like you're still in Vermont. Is that crazy?"

Todd gripped her hand more tightly. "No. I miss you all the time, too," he admitted.

Neither of them was smiling anymore. They both knew that it was going to be a challenge to find enough time to be with each other. Elizabeth could only hope that Todd would try just as hard as she was going to in order to make their relationship work.

"Hey," Dominique Roy said, putting her foot on the brake pedal of her blue Alfa Romeo and pointed out the car window. "Isn't that Todd Wilkins coming out of that restaurant, Courtney? Who's that blond he's with?"

Courtney Kane flipped her mahogany-brown hair over her shoulder and sneered in Todd's direction. "Don't even say that name around me," she snapped. "As far as I'm concerned, Todd Wilkins does not exist. And as for the

43

blond," she added scathingly, "I wish all the trouble on that girl she deserves!"

Courtney stared straight in front of her. She could feel her cheeks burning with anger. She still couldn't believe the misery and humiliation Todd Wilkins had caused her. He had actually given up a chance to go out with her, when everyone knew that Courtney Kane had everything.

Courtney wasn't the type to pretend to be modest—she was used to the best: the best school, the best clothes, and the most exclusive clubs, resorts, and vacations. She should have known right from the start that she was way too good for Todd Wilkins. But instead, Courtney had made one of the biggest mistakes of her life. She had tried to get Todd interested in her. She had even managed to finagle an invitation to a huge party at Todd's house, as his date, no less. That was when everything had gotten fouled up.

Courtney had given Todd the benefit of the doubt, assuming that his interest in Elizabeth was just a bad habit she could shake him out of. She had planned to get rid of the competition by performing a little drama at Todd's party, with herself in the leading role, of course.

The plan had been to lure Elizabeth out to Todd's summerhouse, where Courtney would just *happen* to be with Todd. A well-timed embrace was supposed to convince Elizabeth to get lost, once and for all. It would have worked, Courtney thought grimly, if that drippy boyfriend of Elizabeth's, Jeffrey French, hadn't told Todd that the whole thing was a frame and that Elizabeth still cared for him.

It made Courtney furious to remember the whole absurd incident. "Todd Wilkins is a jerk," she seethed. "I can't believe I ever paid him the slightest bit of attention."

Dominique wasn't used to disagreeing with anything that Courtney said. No one at Lovett Academy was. Courtney almost always got her way. "I can't believe he'd rather be with that girl than with you," Dominique said loyally.

Courtney glared at her. "Just put it this way, Dominique: Todd Wilkins is Enemy Number One on my list." She gritted her teeth. "And Elizabeth Wakefield is a close second. I can't wait to figure out some way to get revenge on them both!"

She couldn't believe how angry it made her, seeing the two of them. And the more she thought about the whole Todd-Elizabeth situation, the worse she felt.

Courtney was in such a rotten mood that night at dinner that she could hardly bear to listen as her father and mother talked animatedly about the television station that Mr. Kane owned. Mr. Kane was talking about a new public relations director at the station, and all the promotion ideas the director had. Courtney had completely tuned out and was concentrating on thinking up ways to get back at Todd and Elizabeth when her father turned to her.

"This should interest you, Courtney," Mr. Kane said. "Mr. Wright wants to sponsor a kind of mini-Olympics among schools in this area, both public and private. He's calling it the Battle of the Schools. It's all going to be backed by Kidd, the new tennis shoe company."

"What do you mean, mini-Olympics?" Courtney asked. "Who competes? And what do they win?"

"Ten schools in the area will compete. Different students will qualify for different events, some athletic, some not. There will be an elimination match, after which the two top schools will be chosen, and then at a later date they'll face off against each other to determine which school is the very best." Mr. Kane smiled. "Students from the school that wins will get to be on Kidd's next commercial. But of course the real prize is school pride—knowing your school is the very best." He patted Courtney on the hand. "How do you think Lovett will do?"

Courtney's eyes sparkled. "Lovett will win for sure," she cried. "Daddy, you know our teams are the best!"

"Among the private schools, true," her father said, smiling. "But what about the public schools like Big Mesa and Palisades High? Don't you think you'll have some stiff competition from them or from Sweet Valley High? You know they ranked very high in the state last fall."

"I hate Sweet Valley High," Courtney muttered under her breath.

"What did you say, dear?" Mrs. Kane asked.

"Oh, just that I know we can beat them all, even Sweet Valley," Courtney said confidently. Lovett would cream that stupid public school if she had anything to do with it.

"That's great, Daddy," she continued cheerfully. "Listen, may I please be excused? I want to call Dominique right away and tell her the exciting news."

"Certainly," Mr. Kane said, but Courtney had already gotten out of her chair and was halfway up the stairs.

"You really think we can win?" Dominique asked dubiously once Courtney had told her all about the Battle of the Schools.

"Of course we'll win!" Courtney cried. She dropped her voice. "Even if there was any question, remember whose father owns the station," she said triumphantly.

"Courtney," Dominique exclaimed, "are you saying your father would deliberately let us win, just because you happen to be enrolled at Lovett?"

Courtney sniffed. "I'm not saying anything, Dominique. Just have a little confidence in our school, that's all."

Dominique was quiet for a minute. "I suppose this doesn't have anything to do with Todd Wilkins and his blond girlfriend," she teased her friend.

"No, it's not related at all," Courtney said innocently. Then she let out a tiny giggle. "Dominique, we're going to humiliate them!"

"Jessica!" Elizabeth exclaimed, standing in the doorway to her sister's bedroom. She stared at her twin. "What on earth are you doing? Don't you realize it's Friday night?"

Jessica had her stereo headphones on and was tapping a pencil against her chemistry book in time to the music. "What did you say?" she asked, taking off the headphones.

When Elizabeth repeated her question, Jessica

48

shrugged. "I have some studying to do," she told Elizabeth.

"Studying? On a Friday night? Jess, are you feeling all right?"

Jessica gave a long, sad sigh. "I can't believe you, Elizabeth. How do you think I'm going to learn one single thing about electromagnetic configurations unless I study?"

Elizabeth crossed her arms and studied her sister with interest. "And can you just remind me why you're studying electromagnetic configurations in the first place?"

"Two weeks from tomorrow morning," Jessica intoned dramatically, "just happens to be when the first entrance exam for Lovett Academy is being given. I signed up for it today, which means I have exactly fourteen days left to learn everything I possibly can."

Elizabeth shook her head in disbelief. "What's happened to my twin sister?" she moaned. She leaned over and touched Jessica's forehead, pretending to check for a fever. "Maybe you have a temporary chemical imbalance in your brain," she said.

"I can tell you all about chemical imbalances," Jessica said cheerfully, opening up her textbook.

Elizabeth covered her ears. "Never mind!"

she said. "Does this mean you don't want to come roller-skating with Todd and me?"

Jessica gave her a withering stare. "Are you kidding?" she demanded. "Tell Todd that in a matter of weeks I'll be at Lovett Academy with him. We can roller-skate across the campus then."

"I think you're crazy," Elizabeth muttered as she left the room.

She hoped Jessica wasn't really going to go ahead with her attempt to transfer to Lovett. But if Elizabeth knew anything about Jessica, it was that once she got an idea in her head, nothing on earth could change her mind.

Five

"Why do you think they called an assembly?" Jessica asked. She and Elizabeth were walking with a big group of friends toward the auditorium, where the mid-morning assembly would be held.

Elizabeth shrugged. "I have no idea. Maybe something special is up."

It was Monday morning, and Elizabeth couldn't help wishing that Todd were at school with her, like in the old days. It seemed silly to miss him, but she did. They had had such a great weekend together, and she couldn't help daydreaming a little as she followed her sister into the auditorium.

"Earth to Elizabeth," Enid teased her when they took their seats.

51

"All right, all right," said Elizabeth. She knew she was going to have to try extra hard to concentrate in school today.

The principal, Mr. Cooper, who was affectionately known as "Chrome Dome" Cooper because of his balding head, got up to address the student body. "Coach Schultz and I have called this assembly today because a very special event is going to be taking place over the next few weeks, and we'd like you all to know about it so you can take part."

"Maybe the 'special event' is that his hair is going to grow back," Amy Sutton whispered to Jessica, who started to giggle.

Coach Schultz received a much warmer round of applause than the principal had. "What we want to tell you about is a special competition called the Battle of the Schools. Ten area schools are being invited to compete, and Sweet Valley High is one of them," the coach said.

"There will be several different events. Some will be traditional sports events—swimming, running, track and field, tennis. There will also be relay races, obstacle courses, and things of that nature. And, finally, part of the competition will consist of a spelling bee and a mini College Bowl." Coach Schultz cleared his throat. "Any students interested in being involved in these events should sign up right away. Different teachers will coach different events, and teams will be selected either by lottery or by tryouts."

The whole auditorium was buzzing with the news. "This sounds great," Amy said enthusiastically. "I wonder what the winning school gets."

"The competition is being run by WXCY and the Kidd tennis shoe company," Coach Schultz continued. "The winning school gets to pick a team of students to be on Kidd's tennis shoe commercials. And more importantly, the school gets a trophy and the pride of knowing it's the very best."

Everyone cheered. "Yea, Sweet Valley High!" a bunch of guys in the crowd called out.

"I wonder if Lovett's in the competition," Amy said suddenly. She turned and looked at Jessica accusingly.

"If they are, I can't possibly be on a team," Jessica announced. "In fact, I should be on the Lovett team if I'm on one at all."

"Traitor," Lila sneered.

"They wouldn't have private schools competing with public ones," Elizabeth argued, hoping she was right. She didn't like the thought of having to compete against Todd.

But Coach Schultz, who was describing each event in greater detail, went on to tell them which schools would be competing. Lovett Academy was first on the list. Big Mesa and Palisades High were also on the list, along with six other area schools.

"Here's what we're going to do," he continued. "There will be two rounds of competition. A qualifying round will be held a week from this Thursday. Both meets will be held at Lovett because they have such good sports facilities and fields."

A few people hissed at the mention of Lovett, but everyone else clapped and cheered at the news. Coach Schultz put up a hand to silence the crowd. "Between now and Thursday we have a lot to do. We need to select teams, practice events, and get ready for the qualifying meets. On Thursday all ten schools will compete in all of the events. The two schools that come out on top will face off two days later, on Saturday. Now, let's just make sure that Sweet Valley High is one of those two final schools!" he yelled.

The audience started to cheer again, and it took several minutes for the coach and the principal to quiet people down enough to explain where to sign up for which events.

"I can't wait," Amy declared when the assembly was over. "We're going to kill all those other schools!" Her eyes were shining with excitement. "I want to make sure I get to compete in a really good event."

"I think I want to do the relay race," Elizabeth said. "The spelling bee and College Bowl sound interesting, too, but it might be more fun to be part of an athletic team."

Jessica sighed. "I'm not going to be on any team," she said sadly. "How can I possibly compete for Sweet Valley High when I'm halfway to being accepted by Lovett Academy as it is?"

"Just you wait, Jessica," Amy snapped. "You're going to be sorry you're not taking our school's side!"

Jessica gave all of her friends a haughty look. "You're the ones who are going to be sorry," she retorted.

She didn't intend to stand around exchanging jeers with them for long, Jessica thought. She didn't see the point. She couldn't wait to start hanging out with the juniors at Lovett—they had to be more mature than this crowd!

"What's wrong?" Enid asked Elizabeth. The two girls had taken their lunches outside to the patio adjoining the lunchroom so they could enjoy their meal in the warm sunshine.

"I'm just a little down, that's all," Elizabeth said. It was Wednesday, and for the past two days Elizabeth had been trying to throw herself into the excitement of trying out for teams for the Battle of the Schools. She also had had her hands full with newspaper work and homework. But, all the same, she missed Todd during the days.

"I wish I felt better about Todd going to Lovett," she confided to Enid. "The few people I've met from that place all seem a little snobby to me, so it's hard for me to get excited when Todd tells me about them or asks me to do things with them." She sighed. "I think he feels I'm not really giving them a chance, that I'm more comfortable with my friends than with his."

"Is that true?" Enid asked quietly. "Maybe he's got a point, Liz."

Elizabeth shook her head, then took a bite of her sandwich. "I've asked Todd to include me in some Lovett activities, so I can get to know some of his friends better. But I haven't met anyone there who I think I could be friends with. That may be my fault, or it might just be that I haven't spent enough time there."

"Well, it's all still so new. Things will get easier after a while," Enid commented.

Elizabeth nodded. She was sure Enid was right. In fact, she was looking forward to getting a chance to spend more time with some of Todd's new classmates. That afternoon was going to be a great opportunity, since she and Todd had made plans to go to a beach close to Lovett and Elizabeth was going to pick him up at school.

Elizabeth parked the Fiat outside the imposing gates that bordered Lovett Academy. She still couldn't get over how beautiful the grounds of the exclusive private school were. As she strolled down the palm-dotted paths, she couldn't help admiring the well-dressed and elegant students. They looked so much older than her friends at Sweet Valley High.

Todd was waiting for her in front of the fountain in the middle of campus. When she walked up, he gave her a big, warm hug and a kiss.

Elizabeth pulled back, laughing. "It's good to see you, too," she said.

She was about to embrace him again when she saw a dark-haired girl approaching them. It was Courtney Kane, the girl who had made such a play for Todd when he first moved back to Sweet Valley.

Elizabeth glanced apprehensively at the beautiful girl. There was no denying that Courtney was intimidating. Her glossy mahogany hair fell around her shoulders, framing a face with high cheekbones and pretty, dark brown eyes. At first it appeared that Courtney was going to walk past without saying a word. Then, at the last minute, she stopped right in front of them. She stared coldly at Elizabeth.

"Well, well, well. What are *you* doing in this part of the world, Elizabeth?" Courtney asked, looking Elizabeth up and down. "What a sweet little outfit," she added. "I didn't know you could find skirts that length anymore."

Todd kept his arm around Elizabeth and gave Courtney a reproachful look.

"I just wanted to remind you, Todd, that Saturday is the big pool party my dad is throwing at the Cedar Springs Country Club. Polo, golf, tennis, the whole works," Courtney explained, smiling at him and ignoring Elizabeth. "I know Daddy is counting on you to come."

"Can I bring a date?" Todd asked, squeezing Elizabeth's shoulder.

Courtney raised her eyebrows and glared at Elizabeth. "Well," she said coldly, "I don't really know. Daddy said something about having to restrict the number of people this year because the dining room is so small."

"Oh, well," Elizabeth said hastily, finding Courtney's behavior so unpleasant, she only wanted to bring the conversation to an end. "I don't really mind, Todd."

But Todd was insistent. "I can't come if Elizabeth can't," he said.

"Then by all means bring Elizabeth," Courtney said. Her eyes seemed to be glistening with angry tears, but her tone was cool. "Do you play polo?" she asked Elizabeth.

Elizabeth fought the urge to laugh. Polo? Who did Courtney think she was, the princess of Monaco? "No," she said with a small smile. "But I'd love to watch everyone else."

Courtney gave her another scornful look. "I'm sure there'll be *something* there you know how to do," she said. Then she turned back to Todd, gave him a cozy little smile, and patted him on the arm. "Maybe you and I can play a private game of golf. What do you say?"

Todd's face turned red. "Uh...sure," he mumbled.

"Great! I'll look forward to it," Courtney said. "Goodbye, *Todd*," she called cheerfully as she walked away.

He waited until she was out of earshot, then turned to Elizabeth with an expression halfway between embarrassment and anger. "I can't believe that girl," he began.

Elizabeth bit her lip. "She probably meant to be friendly," she said. It was pretty hard to imagine that Courtney Kane had good intentions, but Elizabeth had to give her a chance if Todd was going to socialize with her.

"Typical Liz," Todd said, giving her a hug. "You always manage to see the best in everyone." He sighed. "Only not even you can see much good in Courtney Kane! That girl really has it in for me. Ever since the night of my party..." He frowned.

Elizabeth wasn't sure what to say. But she didn't want to ruin one of the few free afternoons they had to spend with each other by getting into a serious discussion. "Hey," she said softly, "let's hit the beach. I think you and I deserve to have a wonderful time together."

Todd gave her a big smile, and Elizabeth almost forgot the unpleasant incident with Courtney Kane. But she couldn't help remembering Courtney's cold gaze and wondering what the girl had in store for her and Todd.

Six

"Boy, do I ever wish I were you," Jessica said enviously. She was sitting on the edge of her sister's bed on Saturday morning, watching her get ready for the daylong party at the country club.

Elizabeth made a face as she buttoned up the cream-colored cotton skirt she had bought at the mall the weekend before. "I wish Todd and I were going to spend the day at the beach, just the two of us," she muttered. "I can't stand things like country club parties, Jess. What am I going to say to these people?"

"They're probably all so glamorous," Jessica said, a dreamy expression on her face. "Talk to them about yachting, horses, flying the Concorde to Paris."

"Right," Elizabeth said. "My favorite topics."

"You're so lucky, and you don't even know it! Do you know how many girls would die to be in your shoes?" Jessica asked. "Your old boyfriend moves back to town and just miraculously turns from being a regular guy into being the son of a hotshot executive who lives in a mansion and belongs to an exclusive club and goes to Lovett Academy and—"

"That," Elizabeth interrupted, "is not exactly an advantage, if you ask me." Standing in front of the mirror, she began to brush her hair. "The fact is, I'd give anything to turn Todd back into a regular guy. I love him like crazy, but sometimes I find his fancy new life a little hard to take."

"I'll go in your place," Jessica volunteered.

"That's OK," Elizabeth said dryly.

"I really will!" Jessica cried, warming to the idea. "Come on, Liz. No one will know. I'll have a good time, and you won't be stuck being miserable all day."

"That's really sweet of you, Jess. But don't you think Todd might notice?" Elizabeth giggled. "We may be identical, but I think Todd knows us well enough to know when he's with the wrong Wakefield!"

Jessica pouted for a minute. "Oh, well," she

finally said. "I guess in a few weeks I'll be at Lovett myself, and I won't have to pretend to be you to get to go to fancy parties in Cedar Springs."

Elizabeth shook her head. She just had to accept the fact that there were some things about her sister she would never understand, and this obsession with Lovett was clearly one of them.

Twenty minutes later she and Todd were driving to Cedar Springs in his new car. Elizabeth thought Todd looked great in his khaki pants and striped cotton shirt, but he seemed a little distracted.

He kept fiddling with the compact disc player that was built into his dashboard. "This thing isn't working again."

Elizabeth giggled. "Poor Todd. That's the thing about expensive new toys. They don't always work the way they're supposed to."

Todd didn't say anything. He kept fiddling with the player, and Elizabeth shot him a side-long glance. The old Todd Wilkins didn't even have a radio in his car. Was it possible he had forgotten what life was like before his dad's promotion?

"So, who's going to be at the party?" Elizabeth

asked, settling back in the passenger seat. She wished she could get more excited about it.

Todd gave up on the CD player and turned on the radio. "The usual crowd from Lovett."

Elizabeth couldn't tell from the sound of his voice how he felt about the party. Was he dreading it, like she was? Or was he actually looking forward to it?

Todd seemed to read her mind, for he turned to her and commented, "You don't sound very enthusiastic about the whole thing. Is something wrong?"

Elizabeth bit her lip. "Well, I guess I feel a little shy around the Lovett kids. Is that weird?"

Todd shrugged. "I guess not," he said, but he didn't sound like his usual self.

Elizabeth wasn't sure what to say. Todd seemed to be in a bad mood, and she felt it was probably best just to let it go. She didn't want to bicker with him today.

"They're perfectly nice people," Todd continued. "I grant you, a few of them are from very rich families, and they're used to having everything. They come across as sort of conceited, but if you get below the surface, you find out they're just like everyone else. Give them a chance," he said.

Elizabeth tried to sound more cheerful than

she felt. "I'm sure today will be a lot of fun," she said. Actually, apart from seeing Courtney, she had no reason not to look forward to meeting some other students from Lovett. But as soon as they arrived at the parking lot of the club, she felt a pang of misgiving. The Lovett kids seemed to belong to a totally different world. They owned the cars in the parking lot, for one thing—BMWs like Todd's, Mercedes, even a Jaguar or two. They really did have everything money could buy.

A boy in a blue cotton cardigan and madras shorts strolled up to them as they got out of Todd's car. "Hey, Todd," he said, putting out his hand.

"Hello, Campbell," Todd said politely, shaking his hand.

"And who's this?" the boy asked, looking at Elizabeth from head to toe.

"I'm Elizabeth Wakefield," she said, taking his hand.

"The pleasure is all mine," he said in a slick, phony voice, squeezing her hand more tightly. "I'm Campbell Rochester," he announced, acting as though Elizabeth should have known that immediately. "Courtney's date," he added. "I hope you and I will get the chance to talk a little more later." When Elizabeth didn't answer, Campbell winked at her.

Elizabeth dropped her eyes, pretending she hadn't noticed. At that moment her biggest hope was that she wouldn't run into either Courtney or her date again.

The country club in Cedar Springs was very ritzy. The dark mahogany-paneled walls of the main room were covered with pictures of hunting scenes, and huge maroon leather chairs were set up against two walls. Elizabeth was tempted to laugh because it all looked so out of place in Southern California. But everyone else seemed to think the club was terrific. Elizabeth spotted Courtney over on one side of the room, presiding over her group of friends.

"Campbell, come here," she commanded, hooking her arm through his with a quick glance in Todd's direction. She didn't look once at Elizabeth.

"Now, after golf we'll meet back here for lunch. Afterward, we can go swimming," Courtney said, "and then dancing."

Elizabeth looked around her. Some of the kids seemed pretty nice. They were clustered in little groups, laughing and talking. But it was hard to know what to say to any of them. Elizabeth took a deep breath. She wanted to be a good sport, but the thought of playing golf didn't exactly thrill her. She had never played before, and it seemed boring to her.

"How about if I just watch you?" she suggested to Todd as the group slowly moved outside. Everyone started picking up clubs from the pro shop.

"You don't want to play?" Todd asked, looking hurt.

Elizabeth hesitated, thinking that perhaps she ought to try. Then she suddenly saw Ben Orson, a sophomore at Sweet Valley High. She knew him because he had submitted a few articles to *The Oracle*. Ben was dragging a bag of clubs out to the first tee.

"Hi, Ben!" Elizabeth said cheerfully when he passed by within earshot.

Several of the Lovett girls who were standing nearby looked up with surprise, apparently because they had heard her speak to Ben. One of them whispered something to the others, and they all giggled.

Elizabeth was sure she was just getting paranoid. Why would they be talking about her? "What are you doing out here?" she asked Ben.

"I work here as a caddy on weekends," Ben said. "What about you?"

"I guess I'm learning how to play golf," Elizabeth said ruefully.

The girl who had whispered to the others cleared her throat. "Come on," she said loudly. "*We* don't need to stand around talking to the hired help." And with that they walked off, leaving Elizabeth with Ben. She could feel anger welling up inside her.

"You should get going," Ben said, pretending to fuss with the strap on the bag he was carrying.

Elizabeth was so angry she could barely restrain herself. *How dare they?* she thought. How could people speak so rudely to someone, just because he happened to be working for them?

She was about to tell Ben how sorry she was when Todd came over. If he recognized Ben, he didn't show it. "Come on, Liz. We're teeing off," he said.

Elizabeth didn't answer. She felt a lump forming in her throat. How could Todd possibly stand being with these people? And if he liked them, if this was where he really belonged, how could she possibly stand being with *him*?

After that, the party went from bad to worse. What Courtney called a pool party was a far cry from the relaxed parties the Wakefields gave in their backyard. Elizabeth found the club atmosphere stuffy and pretentious. Worst of all, the more she got to know the Lovett students, the less she liked them. The girls were narrow-minded and cliquey, and all they talked about were clothes and money. And the guys were just as bad, going on and on about their new cars or their new synthesizers or whatever else they had recently bought with all their money.

The worst by far was Campbell Rochester. He didn't leave Elizabeth alone all day. In the morning he tried to show her how to hold her golf club. When she got in the pool, he jumped in and started telling her how much he liked her bikini. He was obnoxious, and Elizabeth would have told him so to his face, but she was afraid of upsetting Courtney. Worst of all, Todd was so busy talking to his classmates that he didn't have much time to spend with Elizabeth.

By the time the dancing part of the party began, Elizabeth had lost her patience with Campbell, with Courtney, and with Cedar Springs. She was leaning against the wall, watching everyone dance and wondering where Todd was, when Campbell approached her.

"Why don't you dance with me? Don't you know who I am?" he asked her. She had already turned him down twice.

"No," Elizabeth said calmly.

71

"Well, I'm Campbell Rochester the Fourth. My father is Wilson Rochester," he told her.

Elizabeth just looked at him. "Oh," she said. She had no idea who Wilson Rochester was, and she didn't really care to find out.

"Haven't you heard of the Rochester Advertising Group?" he demanded.

"Listen, I have to go," Elizabeth said, starting to walk away.

Campbell grabbed her arm. "Don't go! You're the only girl at this party I really want to talk to!"

Elizabeth shook her arm loose and pulled away, noticing with horror that Courtney was standing in front of them, her mouth set in a tight little line.

"Excuse me," Elizabeth said, pushing past her and scanning the patio for Todd.

"You're excused," Courtney sneered. Elizabeth shivered. She had the distinct impression that whatever irritation Courtney had felt for her before this party had quickly turned into real hatred. She could feel Courtney's icy gaze following her as she crossed the patio, searching for Todd.

Fortunately she found him quickly. He had gone off with Sheffield to look at athletic trophies in the club's display case.

Seeing Elizabeth approach, Todd smiled warmly. "Liz!" he exclaimed, pulling her to him and giving her a hug. "I've been looking everywhere for you."

Elizabeth felt a flood of relief. Todd's arms circled her waist. "Are you having a good time?" she whispered in his ear.

Todd shrugged, then shook his head. "Not really," he whispered back. "You up for leaving? We could drive to the Dairi Burger and get some real dinner."

Elizabeth smiled at him. The dinner Courtney had organized was mostly salads, with some small, elegant hors d'oeuvres that hadn't exactly been filling.

"You sure you don't want to stay longer?" Elizabeth asked.

Todd laughed. "I'm sure. Let's just thank Courtney and take off."

"We really had a good time," Todd told Courtney, who was staring at Elizabeth during the thank-yous with an expression of barely disguised contempt.

"Good, I'm *so* glad," Courtney said in a thin, artificial voice. "See you on Monday, Todd."

"Well," Elizabeth said when they were safely inside Todd's car, "at least I learned how to tee off."

Todd looked at her for a minute and then started to crack up. "It was pretty terrible, wasn't it?"

Elizabeth nodded. She couldn't believe how relieved she was to hear that Todd had had a rotten time, too.

"Phew," Todd said as he put his key in the ignition. "I'm glad you felt the same way I did about the whole thing."

You're not the only one, Elizabeth thought. Todd seemed much more like his old self now— easygoing and relaxed.

And the rest of the evening more than made up for the long, rotten day. They relaxed, ate hamburgers and french fries, told jokes, and exchanged stories about the people at the party. Elizabeth could hardly believe she had been so worried about Todd's reaction to the country club.

Seven

"I can't wait to tell Lila about the party you went to in Cedar Springs on Saturday," Jessica said excitedly. "She's going to die when she finds out Campbell Rochester was there." The twins were driving to school on Monday morning—or, rather, Elizabeth was driving, and Jessica was trying to put on her mascara. The car jerked slightly as Elizabeth shifted gears to make a left-hand turn. "Take it easy, Liz. I almost got this in my eye," Jessica complained.

"Sorry," Elizabeth apologized. "You know, Jess, that party wasn't so great. Some of the kids were pretty nice, but I have to admit that overall I felt uncomfortable with them. Some of them seemed really unfriendly."

"Oh, Liz, you probably just didn't understand them, that's all." Jessica tucked her mascara back inside her purse. "I can tell just from reading the catalog that the people at Lovett have really solid values."

Elizabeth shrugged. She knew better than to argue with her sister about the merits of Lovett Academy. "Well, I didn't get along with all of them, anyway. I don't think Todd had a very good time, either. I'm sort of glad, because to tell you the truth I was starting to feel . . ." Her voice trailed off, and she could sense Jessica's gaze sharpening.

"You sound a little worried," Jessica observed. "Don't tell me you and Todd aren't getting along!"

"No, we're fine," Elizabeth insisted. "In fact, we ended up having a really good time for the rest of the weekend. It's just that sometimes" —she sighed—"I get this nagging little feeling that ever since his father's promotion, Todd's values are changing. He talks a lot more about money than he used to. He told me yesterday at the beach that he wants to learn how to play polo! This is Todd, who used to say any sport but basketball was out of the question. He—" Elizabeth paused for a moment. "Never mind," she said at last.

Jessica looked at her twin. "Uh-oh. Maybe you two are spending too much time together."

Elizabeth laughed. That was always Jessica's first idea, since her idea of "going steady" was seeing the same guy for two dates on the same weekend. "I don't think so," Elizabeth told her sister. "Actually, it's really difficult for us, being at different schools. We don't spend nearly as much time together as we did when he was at Sweet Valley High."

Jessica shrugged. "Well, just make the most of it, then," she advised.

Elizabeth pulled the Fiat into the school parking lot. "Hey, today's the day we find out the teams for the Battle of the Schools," she reminded her sister. "Which one do you want to be on?"

"None," Jessica said, frowning. "I told you, I don't want to be part of any of it, not when I'm thinking about switching schools. It's too hard deciding which school to be loyal to."

Elizabeth shook her head as she turned off the engine. "I can't believe you, Jess. How can you possibly feel loyal to Lovett? You haven't even taken any of the entrance tests yet."

"I still think Lovett's going to win!" Jessica said cheerfully, jumping out of the car before Elizabeth could say another word.

Elizabeth picked up her books from the

backseat and got out of the Fiat. She honestly didn't think her sister knew what she was getting into.

Tryouts and sign-ups for the Battle of the Schools teams had been going on throughout the previous week, and the coaches and teachers had met over the weekend to make final decisions. Coach Schultz had promised he would post the lists of teams up on the bulletin boards in the front hall of the school Monday morning, along with the locations and times of the first practices. Students from all classes could participate in the competition. When Elizabeth walked into school, there was a big crowd in the front hall, and everyone was trying to see who had been selected.

Winston Egbert, who had pushed his way up to the bulletin board, began to announce the names of the contestants. Not surprisingly, Bruce Patman and Kristin Thompson were paired as Sweet Valley's mixed doubles tennis team. Bruce, who was a senior, was the best player on the boys' tennis team, and Kristin was on the pro circuit. Bill Chase, a junior, had been chosen to represent Sweet Valley High in the swimming competition. Aaron Dallas and Shelley Novak would compete in the track and field events. The College Bowl team consisted of Patty Gilbert, Peter DeHaven, and Winston Egbert. Olivia Davidson had been chosen for the spelling bee.

"Who's on the relay team?" Robin Wilson asked Winston, craning her neck for a glimpse of the list.

"You are," Winston told her with a grin. "You, Ken Matthews, Liz Wakefield—and Jeffrey French."

Silence fell over the group clustered in front of the bulletin board. Elizabeth stared down at the floor. Jeffrey, who was standing nearby, looked over at her. She was unable to look up and meet his gaze.

She couldn't believe it. What were the odds of that happening—of the two of them ending up on the same team? He walked over to her, and Elizabeth could tell that he felt as awkward as she did about it.

"Well, I guess we'll be spending a lot of time together over the next few days," Elizabeth said softly, hoping to diffuse some of the tension.

"Yeah, I guess so," Jeffrey muttered.

In the background Elizabeth could hear Robin and Ken animatedly discussing their practice schedule. She felt so embarrassed, she hardly knew what to say or do. How on earth were she and Jeffrey going to handle being on the same team?

* * *

That day after school the first practice for the Battle of the Schools was being held on the Sweet Valley playing fields. Elizabeth had planned to meet Todd in the parking lot, but that was before she learned what team she would be on and with whom. She had asked him to come watch with her, since he didn't have basketball practice that afternoon. She knew how eager Todd was to see his old school buddies, especially Winston and Ken.

But now she wished she could keep him as far from the playing fields as possible. She wasn't looking forward to an embarrassing encounter between Jeffrey and Todd, even though the last time they had seen each other they had parted as friends.

"I have to go to practice out on the track," Elizabeth told Todd when he arrived. She tried to put Jeff out of her mind. "I got chosen to be on the relay team, and our first meeting is today."

"What do you mean, you're on the relay team?"

"You know, for the Battle of the Schools competition. I got chosen to be on the relay team," Elizabeth told him. She smiled. "Aren't you proud of me? You get to watch your girlfriend

80

run back and forth doing all kinds of zany things."

Todd stared at her. "I can't believe it."

"Why?" Elizabeth asked.

"It's funny, that's all." Todd smiled. "Because I'm going to be on the relay team for Lovett. You and I are going to be in direct competition!"

"You're going to be on the relay team? You're kidding!" Elizabeth exclaimed. The irony of the situation struck her, and she started to laugh. "That's great," she said, tucking her arm through his. "Why don't you come with me now and watch practice? Maybe you can give us a couple of pointers."

Todd looked at her closely. "So it doesn't bother you, the thought of competing with me?"

"Why should it?" Elizabeth asked. She gave him a light punch on the arm. "You'd just better be prepared to lose. Because Sweet Valley High can beat Lovett any day!"

Todd shook his head. "I'll come watch you," he said, "but only so I can spy on you guys and report back to the Lovett team!"

The two walked over to the playing fields, teasing each other and joking.

"Hey, what are you doing here, Wilkins?" Ken cried when he saw Todd. "You're a Lovett guy now. No fair coming over here to check out

the competition—even if she *is* your girlfriend."
He grinned at Todd. "What are you going to
do, steal our secret victory plan?"

Elizabeth giggled. "Come on. Todd wouldn't
do anything like that."

"Yeah?" Ken gave Todd an affectionate shove.
"Traitor. What are you doing at a stuck-up place
like Lovett anyway?" he asked.

Todd shoved him back, and the two boys
wrestled good-naturedly for a couple of minutes until it was time for practice to get started.
Todd sat down on the grass and listened with
interest while they talked about the details of
the relay race.

Jeffrey ran up just as the meeting got started.
"Sorry I'm late," he said, barely glancing at
Elizabeth. Then his gaze fell on Todd. He frowned
but said nothing. Elizabeth kept looking nervously from Todd to Jeffrey, hoping nothing
awkward would happen.

Coach Schultz gave Ken a list of instructions,
and they all tried out the different stages of the
event and decided in what order they would
run.

"We really shouldn't let you watch this, Todd,"
Ken said before they began practicing as a team.
"Would you mind?"

Todd looked hurt. "Come on, Ken. I'm not

going to do anything I shouldn't. I just want to be here to cheer Elizabeth on."

"Well, we can't exactly believe that, coming from a Lovett man," Ken said. "It's not fair if you see the way we run this race before the actual meet."

Elizabeth could tell Todd felt bad about being asked to leave, but he stood up obligingly. "I'll see you later," he said to Ken and Jeffrey. Elizabeth reddened a little when Todd blew her a kiss. She hoped no one else had noticed.

"Just don't go turning traitor on us, Liz," Ken said once Todd had gone. "We want to know everyone on this team is one hundred percent for Sweet Valley High."

Elizabeth felt stung. She couldn't believe Ken would say something like that to her.

"Elizabeth is as loyal as they come," Jeffrey said swiftly.

Elizabeth felt a surge of warmth for Jeffrey. He had no reason to come to her defense.

But Jeffrey was right, Elizabeth thought. Of course, he knew she was loyal to her school. When it came to helping Sweet Valley High win, she would do everything she could!

Even if it meant competing against Todd.

"Listen," Todd said. He and Elizabeth were at his house, curled up on the couch next to each other, watching TV. Todd touched the remote control, and the screen faded to black. "I've been thinking about it ever since this afternoon, and I feel kind of weird about the whole relay race thing."

"Why?" Elizabeth asked, surprised. "It's only a game, Todd. It's not serious."

"But, well, it is. Only because you and I—we don't do stuff like this, compete against each other. That's one of the things I like best about our relationship." Todd looked worried.

"We'll just have to make sure we don't let it get to us," she said.

"No, Liz, I mean it," he persisted. "Couldn't you switch and do something else? Or just bag it altogether and come cheer for me?"

Elizabeth stared at him. "What? You want me to quit the team and come give *you* support? Todd, you've got to be kidding," she said. "I don't believe you."

Todd was quiet for a minute. "Actually, I *was* kidding," he finally admitted. "But I don't like the tone of voice you're using, Liz. What if I hadn't been joking? Would it be such a big thing to ask?"

"Yes," Elizabeth said stubbornly, "it would. Why should I quit? Why don't you?"

"Liz, I can't believe how defensive you've

been lately. You don't have to make an issue out of every little thing I say."

"Well, *you* don't have to act like Lovett's so much better than Sweet Valley High all the time," Elizabeth said angrily. "If anyone should quit, it's you, because you have no business competing against Sweet Valley High." She could feel her eyes brimming with tears. Ridiculous as it seemed, the subject was really upsetting her.

"Let's just drop it," Todd said, hitting the "on" button of the remote control.

Elizabeth didn't answer. They could drop it for now, but she wasn't going to forget the argument. And she could tell Todd wasn't, either.

Eight

On Tuesday evening Elizabeth was supposed to meet Todd at the Dairi Burger for a quick postpractice hamburger. Elizabeth was in a somber mood as she waited for Todd at the popular hangout. She'd had an unsettling dream about him the night before, and all day she had wished that they could be together so he could make her feel better. As a result, she had placed more importance on their date than she ordinarily would have. Todd was supposed to meet her at seven o'clock, and by seven-fifteen he still wasn't there. Elizabeth couldn't relax. She was sitting at their regular booth, and she couldn't help tapping her fingers anxiously on the table. She glanced at the clock on the wall again. Seven-twenty. Where was Todd?

By seven-thirty Elizabeth was sure she had made a mistake. Todd was never this late, and he knew she had a ton of homework to catch up on. She was just about to get up to call him when the door swung open and he walked in.

"Hi," he said, walking over to the booth and giving her a quick kiss on the cheek. "I hope your practice was as good as ours was," he added cheerfully, shrugging out of his jacket.

Elizabeth looked at him with surprise as he sat down across from her. "Todd, do you realize how late you are?" she demanded. Her tone was much stronger than she had intended, but the truth was, she felt pretty angry with him.

"I'm sorry," Todd said nonchalantly. "Practice just took longer than I thought it would, and I couldn't think of a way to get a message to you here."

Elizabeth wanted to believe Todd. Maybe she was making too big a deal out of half an hour. "Well, anyway," she said, taking a deep breath, "how are you? How was your day?"

"Great! I got my CD player fixed. And I went riding with Sheffield and some of his friends." Todd's eyes were shining with excitement. "I'm really starting to like it at Lovett. Today I met this guy whose mother is a diplomat at the

French embassy. And his girlfriend is Jacqueline Livingston—you know, of Livingston Pictures? They just got their picture in the paper as one of L.A.'s hottest young couples. Pretty cool, huh?"

Elizabeth raised her eyebrows. She couldn't believe her ears! Todd never used to care about celebrities or "important" people. Was this the same Todd Wilkins she had known and loved for a long, long time?

Todd brought food back to the table. As they ate he went on and on about Lovett—the spring trip to China, the fabulous new computer center, the extensive sports facilities. Elizabeth thought he was starting to sound a little bit like a tour guide.

"Listen, let's change the subject," Elizabeth said, trying to keep her voice light. "Tell me about *you*. You and I haven't talked—I mean really talked—in ages."

Todd looked surprised. He seemed to take her comment as a reproach. "We *were* talking," he pointed out. "I was just trying to tell you a little bit about my life, Liz. Just because you hate Lovett and don't want to hear anything about it—"

"I don't hate Lovett," Elizabeth argued. "Todd, listen—"

But Todd was getting more tense by the minute. "I don't feel like listening, Liz. Not if it means hearing you complain about Lovett one more time. Don't you realize how important it is to my family that I'm there? It would kill Dad if I didn't fit in and make friends."

Elizabeth just stared at him. Somehow she couldn't imagine Mr. Wilkins really caring that much whether or not Todd fit in at Lovett. But she knew it wasn't her place to argue about what his parents thought or felt.

"You have no idea how much pressure I'm under," Todd said. "Everyone expects me to just magically adjust to this whole new lifestyle. It happens to be pretty tough, Liz. And I'd appreciate a little more support from you, instead of all this grief you keep giving me about Lovett."

Elizabeth felt tears spring to her eyes. "I can't believe you!" she cried. "Why are you feeling sorry for yourself? Because you have to get used to having your own screening room and a mansion to live in and a brand-new BMW? I don't think it's your parents who care so much about Lovett Academy," Elizabeth continued, unable to repress her anger anymore. "Let's be fair, Todd. You like being at Lovett. And you can't blame it on your parents."

Todd gripped the edge of the table, his knuckles turning white. She had never seen him this angry before. "Cut it out, Liz. I mean it. Cut it out right now."

Elizabeth hadn't meant to hurt him. The words had just slipped out. But she *did* feel as if Todd's values had changed. And she loved him too much not to speak her mind. "I have to tell you how I feel," she said weakly.

"Well, I'm sick of you judging me," Todd snapped. "You know what? Maybe we should stop seeing each other," he said. "At least till we've figured out what we both want, since all I seem to do lately is disappoint you."

"Stop seeing each other?" Elizabeth repeated. She felt as if the world were tilting beneath her. "Are you sure that's what you want?"

Todd looked stricken, as if he couldn't believe the words had come out of his mouth. "I don't know," he said. "I just know I can't stand fighting with you, Liz. If this is how it's going to be, arguing all the time, then maybe we should break up. From what you've been saying, it seems like that's what you really want."

Elizabeth felt a queasy sensation in her stomach. It wasn't what she wanted at all. But now that Todd had broken up with her, she wasn't going to beg him to take her back.

After all, she had her pride. At the moment it

felt like that was *all* she had. And it didn't give her a whole lot of comfort.

"I can't believe it," Enid said, shaking her head. The two girls were heading out to the playing fields on Wednesday after school—Elizabeth to practice, Enid to watch. "You two really broke up? Liz, that just seems impossible."

"Well, it's not. It definitely happened," Elizabeth said bleakly. "I don't know how exactly. We were having a stupid disagreement that just got bigger and bigger, and then he was saying he wanted to break up with me."

"Can't you try to work it out?" Enid asked. "You two are so much in love with each other."

Elizabeth gave her a desperate look. "Please," she said, "don't remind me. I'm trying to do my best to forget that fact." But Todd had been on her mind all day long, from the second she woke up that morning.

Enid looked at Elizabeth with concern. "Well, good luck with practice," she said.

Elizabeth could see Ken, Robin, and Jeffrey over on the other side of the field. "I'd better get going," she said. She gave Enid an impulsive hug. "Thanks for listening to my sad story."

Enid's eyes were filled with compassion, and Elizabeth knew her friend guessed just how terrible she was feeling. "Take care, Liz. I'll call you tonight," she promised.

"OK, everybody," Ken said when Elizabeth reached the group. "We need to start getting it together today. I think the best plan will be to work individually on the different parts of the relay before trying to put them together. Does that sound good to the rest of you?"

Everyone nodded, and they divided up according to who was doing what in the relay: Jeffrey and Robin had the three-legged race, Ken was running a short sprint while balancing an egg on a spoon, and Elizabeth was left with the rope-climb.

"Not exactly my strongest skill, but I'll do what I can," she said, trying to be enthusiastic no matter how upset she felt.

"Come on," Ken said, clapping his hands together. "Let's get going. We have to make sure we're one of the two schools that comes out on top!"

"Even better," Jeffrey said, a determined expression on his face, "we have to make sure that whatever happens, we're the winners!"

Courtney Kane hated the whole idea of relay races. She thought they were stupid, and she couldn't stand wearing boring old gray gym shorts. She was glad she wasn't competing in the Battle of the Schools. It was so much classier, she thought, to be a spectator than it was to run around carrying an egg on a spoon.

That afternoon she had come out to watch the team practice and was sitting on her jacket on the grass so that she wouldn't get grass stains on her new silk pants. It was kind of fun watching the Lovett team practice, she thought, especially since it meant she could needle Todd Wilkins. For a minute or two, she watched Todd running. "You seem to be putting a lot of effort into this," she said coldly as he passed her. "Doesn't it bug you, competing against that sweet little girlfriend of yours?" She made sure she emphasized the word *sweet*, so that Todd would know what she really meant was that Elizabeth was hopelessly boring and unsophisticated.

Todd didn't respond to Courtney's jibe.

Courtney couldn't blame him for being so slow to defend Elizabeth Wakefield. After all, what good could he possibly say about her? She was clearly the wrong girlfriend for him.

Suddenly Courtney felt she ought to give Todd another chance. Elizabeth was the one she really despised, anyway. "You know," she said loudly, "Daddy gave me tickets to the Lakers game next week. Would you like to come with me?"

"Maybe," Todd said. He looked more concerned with checking out the relay course.

Courtney couldn't believe how rude Todd was sometimes. She stood up and hurried over to the tennis courts, where Dominique was practicing her serve against a backboard.

"It looks like Todd and I have a date," Courtney told her. She filled Dominique in on her recent conversation with Todd—with a few additions to make it more interesting, of course.

Dominique was skeptical. "What about Elizabeth? Maybe he's going to make you get her a ticket, too."

"Don't be silly," Courtney scoffed. "He's going to dump her the minute he realizes that she isn't right for his new life. Who knows? Maybe he's even dumped her already."

"Courtney, you're terrible," Dominique said, grinning slyly.

Courtney tossed her hair back over her shoulders. "Don't forget," she warned, "when Courtney Kane wants something, she gets it. And if I decide I want Todd, then I've got him!"

The two girls giggled as they strolled back to the playing field to watch Todd and his three teammates practice the relay race.

"We need to draw lots to see who does what," Roberta Thornton said. "Todd, you go first."

"Rope-climbing," Todd said.

Courtney nodded her head. From then on, she intended to be the most avid fan of rope-climbing at Lovett Academy.

Everyone else chose lots, and the team got ready to run through the events.

"Now, remember," Jonathan Davis, another member of the relay team, instructed them. "Tomorrow's the big qualifying day. I think we're a shoo-in. The other schools to watch out for are Big Mesa, Palisades High, Crestville Academy—and especially Sweet Valley High."

"They don't stand a chance," Courtney said imperiously.

Jonathan raised his eyebrows. "How can you say that, Courtney? With their record in athletics in the state?"

Courtney shrugged. "The competition isn't just for sports, Jon. Besides, I happen to know the owner of WXCY," she added. "And I know there's no possible way that Lovett can lose this competition."

"What are you saying?" Roberta demanded. "Are you saying your dad would fix things so we'd win?"

"Of course not," Courtney said quickly, realizing her blunder. "I just know we'll win, that's all." She gave Roberta a dirty look. "Can't you have a little school spirit for once, Roberta?"

Todd cleared his throat. "Let's get started." He brushed past Courtney as he headed over to the practice ropes. She smiled sweetly at him. Now that she thought she had another chance with him, she was more than ready to pour on the charm again.

"Good luck, Todd! I'll be rooting for you!" she cried.

"Did you see that look he gave me?" she asked Dominique an instant later. "He won't be with that Wakefield girl much longer, I guarantee you."

"Darn!" Elizabeth exclaimed, frowning up at the rope. Jeffrey had come over to hold it steady for her, but she still didn't see how she was going to manage to climb it. "There aren't even any knots or anything to use for footholds," she said. The rope was tied to a wooden frame shaped like a football goal post, and Elizabeth had to climb to the top, slide to the bottom, touch the ground, and then run to the finish line.

"I guess that's how rope-climbing works," Jeffrey said diffidently.

Elizabeth tried backing off a few steps and rushing up to the rope. By the third try she managed to get several feet up it before she dropped back down to the grass.

"It's a lot harder than it looks," she said sheepishly.

Jeffrey laughed. "Try once more. Here, I'll hold it down tight. The trick is to kind of shimmy up, using one hand at a time."

Elizabeth glanced at him as she backed off to try for one more rushing jump. Was it her imagination, or was Jeffrey being just a tiny bit friendlier than before?

Jeffrey's suggestion worked. With effort, Elizabeth managed to get halfway up the rope this time. The rest of the relay team cheered her wildly when she finally managed to reach the top a few tries later.

"We're going to be fantastic tomorrow," Ken said, slapping Jeffrey on the back. "I'm sure we'll be one of the top schools."

"Yeah," Jeffrey said, sighing. "Lovett's the only school we have to worry about. They're really good. And they've got such fantastic sports grounds and facilities and coaches and stuff..."

"Well, we've got the psychological edge," Ken said, grinning. "Right?"

Elizabeth felt her stomach knot up. She had

managed to forget about Lovett the whole time they were practicing. Now all the dreadful events of the past couple of days came back to her in a rush.

She wondered where Todd was right now. Was he practicing for the Battle of the Schools? Was he thinking about her at all?

Probably not, she told herself. He was probably glad it was all over between them. Now he would be free to spend all his time doing what he said his parents wanted him to do—being with the right people, going to the right parties . . .

She just wished that either she could stop thinking about him or that she could see him again and everything could be the way it used to be.

"Come on, Liz. You have a rope to climb! You're doing great!" Ken encouraged her, leaning over and squeezing her arm affectionately.

Elizabeth turned away, her lower lip trembling as she fought to hold back the tears. Then she backed up and made a mad dash for the rope, hoping none of them would see the emotion on her face.

Nine

"Daddy, you're going to be at the elimination rounds tomorrow, aren't you?" Courtney asked her father that night at dinner.

Mr. Kane took a bite of steak. "Of course I am," he told her. "I'm one of the judges, remember?"

As if she could have forgotten! "Who are the other judges?" Courtney asked casually, pretending to concentrate on her salad.

"Saul Robinson and Dale Carter," Mr. Kane said, naming two of his colleagues at the station.

Courtney bit her lip. "Daddy, you know how important it is for Lovett to win tomorrow, don't you?" she asked.

Mr. Kane sipped his mineral water slowly. "I

certainly do, dear. And I hope you've all been practicing hard," he said calmly.

Courtney didn't think that was much of an answer. It wasn't what she wanted to hear, anyway. "But, Daddy—" she began to protest.

"No *But, Daddy's*," Mr. Kane interrupted. "I hope Lovett wins as much as you do. But this is a competition, fair and square. It's business," he added. To Mr. Kane business was the most important thing of all. "So don't start pouting and expect me to intervene if Lovett is losing."

Courtney grimaced. It had never occurred to her that her father could be so stubborn. And here she had been practically promising her schoolmates they would win!

She glared down at her plate. All she wanted was a guarantee that Sweet Valley High would be humiliated. If her father wasn't going to be the one to provide that guarantee, she would have to figure out some way to make sure on her own.

"Jess?" Elizabeth knocked softly on her sister's bedroom door. It was Wednesday evening, and she had a lot of math homework to catch up on. But she just couldn't concentrate.

Jessica, on the other hand, looked like the very model of a serious student. Books were spread all around her on the bed along with some sample standard examinations.

"Oh, good," Jessica said when Elizabeth walked through the door. "I was just about to come in and ask you some chemistry questions."

Elizabeth groaned. "Jess, do me a favor. Can we talk about something other than studying for once?"

Jessica sighed loudly. "My sister, the lightweight." Then she glanced at Elizabeth again. "Hey, are you all right?" she asked. "You look upset."

"I'm fine," Elizabeth said. "It's just . . ."

"Just what?" Jessica demanded. "You don't look fine at all."

Elizabeth decided to change the subject. "Are you coming to the elimination rounds of the Battle of the Schools tomorrow afternoon?"

Jessica shrugged. "I guess so. I really should be studying, but—"

"Just promise me you won't say the word *Lovett* around me tonight," Elizabeth said abruptly. "I don't think I could stand hearing about that place right now."

"Uh-oh," Jessica said. "Sounds like things haven't gotten smoother with Todd."

"Smoother!" Elizabeth exclaimed. "That's the

understatement of the year. We broke up yesterday," she added miserably.

Jessica's mouth dropped open. "You what?"

"I told you. We broke up," Elizabeth repeated. Her eyes filled with tears.

"Lizzie, that's terrible! Why didn't you come tell me right away?"

"I just couldn't talk about it." Elizabeth shrugged disconsolately. "I made a big mistake thinking that the two of us could get back together and everything would be exactly the way it used to be. Todd's just so different now...."

Jessica jumped up and gave her twin a hug. "So you blew it," she said, patting Elizabeth's shoulder. "Can't you just go back to Jeffrey and tell him you made a big mistake?"

Elizabeth burst into tears.

"Whoops." Jessica patted her on the shoulder again. "I guess I said the wrong thing, huh?"

"I don't...want to...go back to Jeffrey," Elizabeth said between sobs. "Todd's the one I want to be with. Or at least the one I think I want to be with. Only"—she took a tissue from the box on Jessica's bureau and dabbed at the tears on her face—"I'm just so confused."

Jessica sighed. "Maybe you should call Todd.

Tell him you're sorry and you want to talk the whole thing over."

Elizabeth shook her head. "But I'm *not* sorry. Everything I said to him is what I really feel."

"This is beginning to sound like one of the logic problems on the Lovett entrance exams," Jessica commented wryly. "Something's got to give, Liz."

Elizabeth knew her sister was right. But she couldn't call Todd and apologize. How could she tell him she was sorry, when what she was sorry about was that they had lost touch with each other, that he had changed too much to make a go of things?

No, it was hopeless. She was going to have to get used to life without Todd all over again.

"Come on," Amy Sutton said, tugging at Jessica's arm. "I want to watch the relay races."

It was Thursday afternoon, and the Lovett Academy playing fields were crowded with students getting ready to compete in the Battle of the Schools elimination rounds. Jessica was busy admiring the beautifully landscaped campus, and chattering about how great her social life was going to be once she transferred to Lovett. She wasn't the least bit interested in the outcome of the meet. Amy, however, had enough school spirit for both of them.

The playing fields had been divided into three main areas for outside events. The inside events—the College Bowl and the spelling bee—were going to be held in the auditorium. At the end of the afternoon the two schools with the highest points would be identified, and those two would move on to the championship on Saturday.

"Why do you want to watch the relay races so badly?" Jessica asked Amy, craning her neck to admire a passing boy in Lovett colors.

"I have my reasons," Amy said mysteriously.

Jessica shrugged. "OK." She was so busy looking around her that she almost tripped over a root in the ground, and Amy burst out laughing.

Jessica gave her a dirty look. "Just wait till I'm a student here. You'll see."

They both quickened their steps to hurry to the center of the playing fields. At exactly four o'clock the coaches blew their whistles, signaling that the meet was starting. Only one event could be held at a time in order to make room for all ten schools, so Amy and Jessica had to wait awhile for the relay races. By the time it began, Lovett and Sweet Valley High were neck and neck, with Big Mesa and Palisades High next. Lovett had swept most of the track and field competitions, but Sweet Valley High had closed in by winning swimming and tennis.

"Come on, Liz! Come on, Ken!" Amy hollered, jumping up and down and waving a red banner when the Sweet Valley High team appeared on the field. Red and white were Sweet Valley High's colors, and all the relay racers were wearing red-and-white T-shirts. Lovett's colors were blue and gray, and Jessica couldn't help cheering as the Lovett team jogged up to the starting place. Right behind them were the Big Mesa and the Pacific Palisades students.

Each relay team had four members, and the sense of excitement before the qualifying race was infectious as the teammates patted one another on the backs, crouched down, and got ready to go. When Coach Schultz blew his whistle, all ten egg-racers sped down to the finish line and back. Ken's egg wobbled a little bit, but he was the fastest, touching Jeffrey and Robin before any of the others crossed the line. Jeffrey and Robin were terrific at the three-legged race, and by the time it was Elizabeth's turn, Sweet Valley was winning.

"Come on, Todd!" Courtney screamed from the sidelines. Todd zoomed past Elizabeth and climbed the rope with three seemingly effortless lunges. Elizabeth was right after him. When she got back down to the bottom, she touched the ground, then sprinted to the finish line, arriving just after Todd.

Coach Schultz blew his whistle. "That's it!" he cried. Lovett Academy had won the qualifying match, and Sweet Valley High had come in second. The two schools would face off again in two days.

"Good luck!" Coach Schultz cried. "And thanks to everyone for participating today."

Jessica was beside herself with excitement. "What a school," she said. "I can't believe how great they are."

Amy shot her a dirty look. "Jess, I can't believe you're serious about this Lovett business. It's unpatriotic."

Jessica was about to retort when Ken Matthews came over to them, grinning. "Wasn't that great? Sweet Valley really pulled through! And just wait and see what we're going to do to those guys on Saturday!"

Amy was looking at Ken with admiration. "You were great," she gushed. "Where'd you get your egg-racing talent, Ken?"

"Oh, I was just born with it, that's all," Ken said with a smile.

Jessica stared at Amy. She waited until Ken

was out of earshot to start grilling her friend. "I don't support the stupid smile on your face right now has anything to do with Ken Matthews, does it? Is that why you wanted to watch the relay races? You're not interested in him, are you?"

"Really, Jessica," Amy said disdainfully. "Can't I even be friendly to someone without your suspecting something romantic is going on? Besides, I told you I wanted to see Todd and Liz compete against each other."

"Mmm-hmm," Jessica murmured. She didn't believe Amy could be interested in any boy just as a friend.

Elizabeth had rope burns on both hands. She glanced around for her teammates, but they had all moved to the other side of the field. She scanned the area quickly for Todd but didn't see him anywhere, either.

She had been so sure he would hang around afterward and say something to her. *OK*, she told herself, *maybe I haven't called him in the past few days, but why can't he make the first move?*

Elizabeth walked slowly across the field with her head down. She didn't even see Courtney until she almost ran right into her.

"Oh, hi," she said, thinking that Courtney

Kane was just about the last person she wanted to see, especially now.

"Hi, Liz. Nice try on the ropes," Courtney said in a bright voice. "Too bad Todd beat you. Speaking of which, where is he? Didn't he stick around to tell you what a terrific job you did?" She shook her head, making little clucking noises with her tongue. "That wasn't very nice of him."

"I don't know where he is. I haven't seen him," Elizabeth said in a stiff, strained voice. She saw Courtney's eyes light up immediately at this piece of information.

"Really!" Courtney exclaimed. She looked as if she had just been given a winning lottery ticket. "Well, good luck on Saturday," she added in a voice that seemed to suggest she thought Sweet Valley was going to need it. "I see a friend waving to me. Bye!" And before Elizabeth could say another word, Courtney ran off toward the parking lot, where Dominique was waiting for her.

"Liz?" a voice called from behind Elizabeth.

She spun around and found Jeffrey looking at her.

He smiled. "I just wanted to tell you what a great job you did on the ropes today. Thanks for helping get us in the finals," Jeffrey said.

Elizabeth swallowed hard. "Oh, it was nothing," she mumbled. "But, thanks. You were great, too."

Why did Jeffrey have to be so wonderful? He couldn't possibly know it, but the compassionate look on his face right then made her want to throw herself in his arms and cry on his shoulder.

"You need a ride anywhere?" Jeffrey asked, looking thoughtfully at her.

Elizabeth shook her head. "Thanks. I've got my car," she told him.

What she didn't say was that she was still hoping Todd would show up. She wanted him to put his arms around her and tell her that things were going to be just fine between them, despite everything that had gone wrong lately. But that obviously wasn't going to happen. He probably never wanted to see her again. Why else had he disappeared?

Ten

On Friday afternoon Jessica had her first interview at Lovett. It was actually more a chance for her to learn about the school than an interview, according to Mrs. Henry, the admissions officer who had set it up on the phone. They wanted her to come in during the week, and the only way Jessica could manage it was to miss an afternoon of school, since Lovett was almost an hour away by car.

Classes were in session when she arrived, and no one was around, so it seemed even quieter on campus than usual. Not like Sweet Valley High, where her friends were bustling around, teasing one another, calling remarks out in the hallways. Jessica felt a momentary pang, but then she saw a cute guy in the hallway of the administration building, and her spirits lifted. When she transferred, she would meet a lot of exciting new—and rich—guys, she thought. Her social life was going to be a hundred percent better once she enrolled in Lovett!

Mrs. Henry was waiting for her in the admissions office. "Let's take a quick tour before we talk," she said. *Quick* was the word for the tour Jessica received in the next ten minutes. Mrs. Henry talked like a robot. She pointed out the gym, the pool, the dance studio, and the dining hall, all in the same monotonous, cheerless voice. "Of course, all Lovett students use study hall to prepare for college entrance exams," she continued. "We here at Lovett pride ourselves in placing students in the very best colleges in the country."

Jessica gulped. There would be no more horsing around with Lila and Amy during study hall....

"As you know, we require our students to follow a dress code," Mrs. Henry continued. "We do not allow jeans, shorts . . . well, I'm sure you've read all about it in the catalog. There are a number of rules at Lovett, but they only make the academy the fine place that it is."

Jessica couldn't help thinking that Mrs. Henry sounded like a prerecorded message—or a drill instructor at a boot camp. Taking a deep breath, Jessica tried to regain some of her enthusiasm. But by the time Mrs. Henry had told her to take a seat in her stuffy office, Jessica wasn't quite so sure Lovett was as exciting as she had thought it was.

"Now," Mrs. Henry said, placing the tips of her fingers together as she leaned back in her desk chair, "tell me a little bit about *you*. What kind of qualities do you have that make you think you're a Lovett girl?"

"I, uh, I'm very enthusiastic," Jessica began awkwardly.

Mrs. Henry treated her to a cold smile. "Enthusiasm is a nice quality," she said blandly. "What else?"

"I—" Jessica faltered again. What could she possibly say about herself that would convince Mrs. Henry she was Lovett material? She couldn't tell her about cheerleading or the sorority. All that sounded too frivolous. If only Elizabeth were here, Jessica thought. Everything Elizabeth liked to do would be perfect for Mrs. Henry. "I like to write," Jessica blurted out. It wasn't the first time she had impersonated her twin to get herself out of a tight spot!

But to her surprise Mrs. Henry didn't seem at all impressed by her interest in writing. "How nice," she said, opening up Jessica's folder.

"Well, of course, a good deal depends on how you do on your entrance examinations," she said vaguely. "Remember, the first one's a week from tomorrow morning. Bright and early."

Jessica didn't like the sound of that. "I've been studying very hard," she said truthfully.

Mrs. Henry closed the folder. "We'll see next Saturday," she said briskly. "I wish you the best of luck, Miss Wakefield."

Miss Wakefield! Jessica felt a shiver run up her spine. What was she doing in this place? Was she out of her mind to think about leaving a wonderful, laid-back school like Sweet Valley High to come here?

But she had already told everyone that she would be at Lovett next year. If she backed out now, they would all think she was chickening out because of the entrance exams or because she had bombed at the interview. No, she couldn't give up her plan to transfer to Lovett, Jessica decided. Lila and Amy would never let her hear the end of it.

Fortunately, when she left Mrs. Henry's office and headed out the main doors, she felt her enthusiasm rushing back. It *was* a beautiful place. Not only that, but now that the students were outside between classes, Lovett looked a lot livelier. She even saw a couple of drop-dead-gorgeous guys hanging out by the fountain in the middle of campus.

I'm going to love it here, Jessica thought stubbornly.

That is, if she could convince Mrs. Henry and the rest of the admissions council that she was smart enough to fit in!

Jessica was just about to get into her car when she heard someone calling her name.

"Jessica!" Todd shouted, panting as he ran to catch up with her. "What are you doing here in the middle of the day? At first I thought—"

He broke off, but from the look on his face she guessed what he was going to say. He had thought she was Elizabeth, and now he was disappointed.

"I had an appointment with Mrs. Henry, to talk about transferring here," Jessica said.

"How did it go?" Todd asked.

"Oh, fine," Jessica said, trying to sound more confident than she felt. "Mrs. Henry seems to think I'd fit right in here."

Todd squinted out at the parking lot. "Yeah, well...there's a lot to be said for Sweet Valley High," he said. "Hey, how's your sister?" he asked abruptly.

Jessica considered his question for a minute. Should she tell him the truth—that Elizabeth had been slumping around the house too miserable to eat or talk to anyone? Or should she try to preserve a little of her twin's dignity? She opted for the second choice. It was what she would want Elizabeth to do for her. "Oh, she's fine," she said airily. "Pretty busy getting ready for the big event on Saturday. I guess you must be, too, huh?"

Todd shrugged his shoulders. "Yeah, I guess I am," he mumbled. "So, she hasn't talked about me at all? She hasn't said anything to you about me?"

"Why would she?" Jessica asked. She figured she was doing Elizabeth a favor. Why make it easy on Todd? Jessica thought he needed to suffer a little bit.

Todd's face fell. "Never mind," he said.

Jessica had a distinct feeling of triumph. Maybe her meeting with Mrs. Henry hadn't been a complete success, but at least she could tell Elizabeth the good news.

Todd Wilkins missed her like mad!

"Tell me again," Elizabeth begged her.

"I *told* you," Jessica said, aggravated. "How many times can you stand hearing the same thing? Look, Liz. It's obvious you two just had a stupid fight. So call him up and tell him you're sorry. Or tell him you want *him* to be sorry. Just do something—and quit breathing down my neck!"

Elizabeth paced back and forth from one side of her sister's bedroom to the other. "It's been three days since we last talked, and he hasn't called once. Not even a two-second how-are-you-and-are-you-still-alive kind of phone call."

"Oh, come on, Liz! You can call *him*," Jessica reasoned.

"I think he should be the one to make the first move. He's the one who started all the problems," Elizabeth said.

"Very mature attitude, Liz. If I said something like that, do you know what you'd tell me? That it takes more than one person to have an argument."

Elizabeth knew Jessica was right. "All right," she said. "I'm going to do it." And before she could change her mind, she went over to Jessica's extension and punched Todd's phone number.

After four rings, the Wilkinses' answering machine picked up the call.

"Rats," Elizabeth said, hanging up the phone. "They're not home."

"Maybe Todd has a hot date," Jessica teased her.

Elizabeth stared at her in horror. "Do you really think he does?" she cried.

"Liz, you're pathetic." Jessica moaned and covered her ears with her hands. "Listen, I don't have time to listen to cries from the love-lorn. If I don't get some serious studying in, I won't stand a chance of getting into Lovett."

"I can't believe you want to go there, anyway," Elizabeth snapped. "It's a terrible school. I hope that we slaughter them tomorrow!"

When Jessica didn't answer, Elizabeth eyed her closely. "Are you planning on coming to watch?" she asked. "Or is that too much to ask for, now that you're transferring?"

"Of course I'm coming," Jessica retorted. "I just don't know who I'm rooting for, that's all."

"What are you doing?" Dominique demanded. It was Friday night, and the two girls were in Courtney's bedroom. They had just been trying on some of Courtney's newest clothes for an upcoming party at Lovett.

Courtney was busily writing something down in the big spiral notebook she kept next to her bed. "I'm trying to come up with ideas," she said, her eyes gleaming.

"Ideas for what?" Dominique wanted to know.

"Ideas to make sure we win tomorrow. I

120

don't want to take any chances," Courtney said solemnly. "Look, it's just Sweet Valley against us, right? Now, you and I both know that all our teams are better than all of theirs. But just in case something goes really wrong and it looks like they might be getting an edge on us . . ."

"What are you going to do?" Dominique asked suspiciously.

Courtney grinned. "Haven't you ever heard of giving people a little extra assistance? Take the College Bowl, for example. I figure there've got to be plenty of ways we can send signals to Sheffield and Alison. If we stand in a certain place and one of them doesn't know the exact number—"

"But, Courtney, that's cheating!" Dominique protested.

Courtney looked at her friend as if she had lost her mind. "It isn't *cheating*," she said, "it's called helping. There's a big difference."

"Yeah? I don't see it," Dominique argued.

"Don't you want Lovett Academy to win?" Courtney asked. "Come on, Dominique. Don't you realize how high the stakes are? This isn't just a question of winning a contest or getting to be on TV to advertise some stupid sneakers."

"Oh, no?" Dominique asked. "Then what is it?"

"It happens to be a matter of *us* against *them*," Courtney said fiercely. "Don't you see? Sweet Valley High stands for everything we hate. Those kids don't have any class. You remember what happened when Elizabeth Wakefield came to that party at the country club, don't you?"

"Not really," Dominique said. "What happened?"

"You don't remember how she ignored all of us and went straight for that public school kid—that *caddie*—and started talking to him? When she could have talked to any one of a number of kids from really good families?"

"Maybe she just knew that guy from school. Maybe they're friends," Dominique observed.

"Don't be stupid!" Courtney cried. "Elizabeth doesn't care about anybody but herself! She was so busy trying to keep Todd Wilkins's attention that whole day long that I'm surprised she even found time to talk to the hired help!"

Dominique didn't say anything, and Courtney cleared her throat. "So, anyway, the point is that we have to show Sweet Valley High—and the rest of the world—exactly what Lovett

Academy stands for. That's why it's so important we win. *Now* do you see what I mean?"

"I guess so," Dominique said. "I just don't think we should cheat. I think we should try to win fair and square."

"Dominique, sometimes you're so stupid!" Courtney cried. "Who ever wins anything fair and square? You should hear Daddy talk about what it's like being CEO of a big company. People are always trying to cut each other out of deals, steal things, or tell lies about each other. The only way to win is to make sure you play the game better than anyone else."

Dominique looked skeptical, but she kept listening.

"Just promise me you'll do whatever I tell you to tomorrow," Courtney begged her. "I'll take care of everything. Just help me out when I ask you to. Will you?"

Dominique twisted a lock of hair around her finger. "OK," she said at last. "I guess you know more about stuff like this than I do."

"That's right," Courtney said, patting her on the arm. "That's why you're such a good friend, Dominique. You're always willing to help me. I'll tell you what," she added, leaning forward and dropping her voice. "You know that new green sweater of mine you just tried on—the one with the black border?"

Dominique nodded, her eyes shining.

"Well, if you help me make sure Lovett wins tomorrow, I'll give you that sweater. For keeps," Courtney promised.

"All right!" Dominique cried. Then the two girls shook hands to seal the deal.

"Tomorrow is going to be great," Courtney predicted. "It may just be one of the best days of my life!"

Eleven

Saturday was a bright, sunny day, with just a tiny bit of an ocean breeze to cool the air. A perfect day for the Battle of the Schools, Courtney thought, pulling on her jeans. She put on her makeup quickly, brushed her hair, and then raced downstairs. The competition began at nine o'clock, and Courtney wanted to be there early.

After the qualifying meet on Thursday, the coaches had decided that the competition between Lovett and Sweet Valley High would be divided into two parts. In the morning they would hold the College Bowl, the spelling bee, and the swimming and tennis events. Each event was worth ten points, and there were ten events in all. In the afternoon the remaining events would take place, after a short break for lunch. At the end of the day, the team with the most points would be the winner.

Courtney had every intention of making sure that Lovett won everything that morning. She didn't want them lagging behind, and she knew how important it was for morale to stay high. One of the reasons she wanted to get to the playing fields early was to bolster spirits wherever she could.

As luck had it, the first person she bumped into at the Lovett fields was Todd.

"Well, hello," she said when they met. "You're here early. Are you all set for the big day?"

"Yeah, I guess," Todd said unenthusiastically.

"That's the spirit," Courtney said blithely. She gave him a knowing little smile. "Want to go out and celebrate after we win? Daddy says I can take whoever I want out for a big pizza dinner, his treat."

Todd looked at her. "What makes you so sure we're going to win? Sweet Valley High has a lot of terrific athletes, and a lot of really smart students, too."

Courtney thought one of Todd's least attractive traits was his loyalty to Sweet Valley High. It was so tedious the way he went on and on about it. She just hoped he would get over it soon. "Well, I'm sure they'll do splendidly," she assured Todd. "But I still have a lot of faith in Lovett. And in you, Todd."

Todd didn't respond to Courtney's compliment. He was staring across the field at the Sweet Valley High team. They were warming up with some stretching exercises. "See that guy over there?" he said suddenly.

Courtney squinted to get a better view. "Mmm-hmm," she murmured, wondering what Todd was getting at.

"That's Ken Matthews. He's one of the best athletes in the state. He's captain of the football team at Sweet Valley High—and he used to be one of my really good friends," Todd said sadly. "He's on the relay-race team. I feel rotten competing against him."

"Oh, come on, Todd," Courtney said in her brightest voice. "Lighten up. You'll feel better once we win." And before he could drone on about Sweet Valley High, she hurried off to find Dominique.

Honestly, Courtney thought to herself. Todd was incredibly cute, but he could be such a bore sometimes!

The morning got off to a good start for Lovett, with Jake Iser beating Bill Chase in the swimming competition. But Sweet Valley High rallied by winning the tennis mixed doubles, making the two schools even, with ten points each.

Next it was time for the College Bowl. "Come on," Courtney told Dominique as they hurried toward the Lovett auditorium, where the bowl was being held. "You and I have our work cut out for us."

Each school had three students participating in the College Bowl. Sweet Valley High's team consisted of Winston Egbert, Patty Gilbert, and Peter DeHaven. Lovett's team had Sheffield Eastman, a senior named Bradley Tushingham, and a movie director's daughter named Alison deLong. Mr. Smithfield, an old and distinguished history teacher at Lovett, would ask the questions and moderate the bowl.

"Alison knows we're here, ready to give her clues," Courtney whispered to Dominique as they both slipped in behind the heavy brocade curtains at one side of the stage. Courtney pulled a large book out of her shoulder bag.

"What is that?" Dominique demanded.

"Sshh! It's a copy of College Bowl questions and answers." Courtney smiled, obviously pleased with herself. "I told Alison to tell the others. If we move the curtain twice, that means the answer is true. If we tug it only once, it's false."

Dominique looked stricken. "What if we get caught?" she asked.

Courtney shook her head. "Don't worry. We'll be totally out of sight. Now, come on. You have to be ready to help me. We need to look stuff up with the speed of lightning if we're going to be able to help them."

Back in the auditorium, Mr. Smithfield was explaining the rules of the College Bowl to the contestants and their audience.

After adjusting his glasses and peering out at the audience, he said, "I'll start the bowl by asking one of our six contestants a question. If that student answers incorrectly we move on to the other team. If he or she answers correctly, however, the team gets two points, and is then given a follow-up question. Anyone on the team may help with the follow-up—but it is only worth one point. The maximum number of points any team can get in one turn is three. Sweet Valley High will be given the first question. Are the rules clear?" he asked, addressing himself to the bowl's participants. Everyone nodded. "All right, then, let us begin."

The first question went to Winston Egbert. "The highest mountain in the world is Mount Kilimanjaro in East Africa. True or false."

Winston cleared his throat. "Uh ... false," he said.

"Correct," Mr. Smithfield said. "Mount Everest is the highest. All right, here's your follow-up: The summit of Mount Everest was first reached by two explorers, Sir Edmund Hillary and Tenzing Norkay. The year they made their ascent was 1923. True or false."

The Sweet Valley team exchanged glances. Winston shrugged his shoulders, clearly at a loss. Finally Patty Gilbert spoke up. "False" she said.

"Correct!" Mr. Smithfield said with a smile. "It was 1953."

Mr. Smithfield turned to the Lovett team. "Alison, the name of the man who made these words famous—'one small step for man, one giant leap for mankind'—was Neil Armstrong. True or false."

Alison coughed. There was a long silence. Dominique was frantically flipping through the book. "Here, Armstrong ... astronaut who landed on the moon," she told Courtney quietly. "Yes."

Courtney looked triumphant as she leaned forward to move the curtain twice.

"Uh, that's true," Alison said tentatively.

"Correct," Mr. Smithfield said. "And now the

follow-up question. The year Mr. Armstrong made this statement was 1963. True or false."

"False. It was 1969," Sheffield answered quickly, looking delighted with himself. The Lovett half of the crowd cheered loudly. The score was tied, three points each.

Mr. Smithfield put the next question to Patty Gilbert on the Sweet Valley High team, and she got it wrong. The following question went to the Lovett team.

"Bradley, rock and roll singer Bob Dylan's real name is Robert Zimmerman. True or false," the teacher said. Bradley cleared his throat, deliberating.

"*I* know this one," Courtney whispered to Dominique. She stepped forward and gently tugged the curtain twice. "Bradley's such a nerd, all he knows about is physics," she complained.

"True!" Bradley said confidently.

"Correct," Mr. Smithfield said. "Now, this is for the entire Lovett team. One of Mr. Dylan's hit songs claims that 'the answer is blowing in the wind.' True or false."

"True," Alison answered, without glancing once at the curtain.

"That's right," Mr. Smithfield said. "Peter, a

United States senator may serve only two terms. True or false."

"False," Peter answered without hesitation. Then Sweet Valley missed their follow-up question and fell further behind.

"Alison, this next question is yours. Water boils at two hundred and twelve degrees centigrade."

Alison sat there for a minute without saying anything. Then, since she obviously didn't have a clue and needed to stall for time, she asked Mr. Smithfield to repeat the question.

Meanwhile, Dominique sped through the College Bowl book until she found the answer. "False," she told Courtney.

Courtney grinned and gave the curtain a short pull.

"I'm going to say that's false," Alison said slowly, appearing to have given the matter of lot of thought.

"You're right! Water boils at two hundred and twelve degrees Fahrenheit," Mr. Smithfield informed them.

"Hey," Lila said under her breath to Jessica. "These questions are a lot harder than I thought they would be."

Jessica didn't say anything. She was staring

at the side of the stage. She knew she wasn't imagining things. She had definitely seen the curtain twitch just before the Lovett students had given their answers. Was she going nuts, or was somebody standing behind that curtain, giving signals to the team?

For the rest of the College Bowl, Jessica kept a close watch on the curtain. Someone from Lovett was clearly sending signals to the team, because before any of them answered a question, they stared at the side of the stage. They weren't very good actors, either. They pretended to be nonchalant about it, but Jessica figured it out right away.

Strangely enough, no one else seemed to notice. Lovett was pulling way ahead, and Winston Egbert looked ready to weep. But Jessica was the only one watching the curtain— besides the Lovett competitors, of course.

"That's it! The score is twenty to fifteen, Lovett. Lovett has won the College Bowl!" Mr. Smithfield, the moderator, exclaimed fifteen minutes later.

"What are you looking at, Jess?" Lila demanded, shaking Jessica's shoulder. "It's time for the spelling bee. We're supposed to go down to the lecture hall now."

Jessica didn't say a word. Her eyes narrowed,

she was carefully watching as Courtney and Dominique crept out from behind the curtain at the side of the stage and walked down the wooden steps as if they belonged backstage. Nobody seemed to have noticed anything out of the ordinary but Jessica.

Courtney confidently surveyed the auditorium, as if she were daring anyone to confront her. Jessica wasn't sure what to do. Either she told Mr. Smithfield what she had seen—and made waves at the school before she even took the entrance exams to get in—or she kept quiet and let Sweet Valley lose unfairly.

Jessica was furious. If there was anything she hated, it was being caught in a position where neither option felt right.

"What's wrong with you?" Lila asked her. "Come *on*, Jess. You may not care if we beat Lovett, but I do!"

Jessica took a deep breath. It looked like her only choice was to follow Lila to the spelling bee and keep her mouth shut—for now.

Throughout the afternoon the competition between the two schools became more and more intense. Newsmen from WXCY were all over the place, interviewing students and shooting footage of different events. The relay race was going to be the last event of the day, and because the two schools were so closely matched, it appeared that the race might decide the Battle of the Schools.

In fact, this proved to be true. Each school had won four events before track and field, and when the four-hundred-meter race ended in a tie, that gave each school forty-five points.

"This is it," Courtney said grimly, staring at Dominique. "We've got to do something to make sure we win. We can't risk a tie."

Everyone was out on the playing fields, getting ready for the relay race. "Dominique, Courtney, help us set up!" a senior named Bob cried, carrying orange cones to mark the course.

Courtney winked at Dominique. "This just might be our chance," she whispered. She followed Bob to the woodshed where the ropes for the rope-climb were kept.

"Can you drag out two ropes? You'll need to get help—they're heavy," Bob said. "That one is ours, and the other is Sweet Valley's. Be sure not to take out the one in the back. It's rotted through halfway up."

Courtney's eyes widened. "OK," she said. When Bob ran back onto the field, she started pulling on the ropes with all her might. One for Lovett, and the other for Sweet Valley.

135

"Hey," Dominique said, looking confused as Courtney handed her one end of a rope to pull out to Sweet Valley High's course. "Are you sure that's the right one?"

"I know what I'm doing," Courtney snapped, tugging even harder to get the rope out of the back of the shed. She ignored the look of horror on Dominique's face. When it came right down to it, Dominique wasn't a real competitor. She would never be a winner, either. Courtney knew that if you wanted to win you had to be willing to do anything to achieve your goal.

"Everybody ready?" the two coaches cried.

Elizabeth could feel her palms sweating. She glanced nervously over to the spot where Todd was waiting.

To her surprise *he* had been staring at *her*. She quickly looked away.

"On your mark, get set—go!" the coaches cried in unison.

Elizabeth felt her heart pounding as she watched Ken race down to the last cone, the spoon wobbling a little in his hand. He was so good, she thought admiringly. He managed to cover the course and rush back at least five strides in front of the Lovett runner.

The crowd was going crazy. "Go, Sweet Valley High!'' they screamed. ''Go, Lovett! Come on! You can do it!''

Ken ran across the starting line and touched Jeffrey and Robin. They sped across the course with Robin's left leg tied to Jeffrey's right. They moved with such skill and agility that they pulled ahead of the Lovett competitors.

Elizabeth crouched down, ready to go. This was it. They were ahead now, and it was up to her to make sure that Sweet Valley High won the Battle of the Schools.

Twelve

"Come on, Liz! Come on, Liz!" the Sweet Valley High students were screaming at the top of their lungs. And, just as loudly, the Lovett students were cheering for Todd. After he was tagged, he started to race across the field toward the Lovett rope just as Elizabeth began to climb.

Jessica pushed to the front of the crowd, her voice hoarse from screaming. All feelings of divided loyalty were forgotten as she watched her sister begin to shimmy up the rope. All she wanted was for Elizabeth to win.

"Come on, Lizzie!" she screamed at the top of her lungs.

Then Jessica saw something that made her

heart stop. The rope Elizabeth was climbing seemed to be getting thinner and thinner at the top. Jessica craned her neck, trying to see over the person in front of her.

Everything happened so quickly, it was hard to figure out what was going on. But a loud gasp rose from the crowd as Elizabeth's rope broke and she tumbled to the ground with a cry of pain.

"Keep going, Todd!" Courtney cried.

The whole crowd had become quiet when Elizabeth fell, and Courtney's voice was horrifyingly clear. Jessica felt the adrenaline pulsing through her as she pushed her way forward. "Let me through!" she cried, scrambling toward the place on the grass where Elizabeth was lying.

But Todd beat her to it. He was halfway to the top of his rope when he saw Elizabeth fall. Without a second's pause he dropped down to the ground, raced to Elizabeth, and took her in his arms.

Pandemonium broke out on the field as parents and teachers rushed over, and someone shouted to call an ambulance.

But Elizabeth quickly sat up and rubbed her elbow. "I'm fine, I'm really fine," she insisted.

She was talking to Coach Schultz, but her eyes were fixed on Todd's face.

"I don't know how on earth that rope got up there," Coach Schultz said, shaking his head angrily. "Elizabeth, are you *sure* you're all right? You don't feel dizzy? Did you hit your head?"

Elizabeth shook her head. "No, I'm fine," she said again. "I landed on my arm, and it just feels bruised. Really."

Todd held Elizabeth's hand tightly. "Liz," he whispered, "when I saw you fall, when I thought something might have happened to you..."

Elizabeth's eyes filled with tears. All she remembered was a terrible sensation as the rope gave way, and then the fall. And the first thing she had seen when she opened her eyes was Todd's face, filled with worry and tenderness.

Courtney ran to her father, who had come over to check on Elizabeth. She tugged at his sleeve. "What are we going to do about deciding who wins? Daddy, we have to pick a winner!"

Mr. Kane frowned at her. "Not now, Courtney," he reproached her.

Yet now that everyone knew Elizabeth was all right, both teams were eager to finish the competition. "We need another event. Let's have a tug-of-war!" Bruce Patman cried.

This suggestion was taken up with cheers

from the whole crowd. "Tug-of-war! Tug-of-war!" everyone started chanting.

The coaches put their heads together with the judges and a few minutes later announced that a tug-of-war would indeed be the tiebreaking event to end the Battle of the Schools. The relay teams would battle it out, four against four.

"We need a replacement for Elizabeth," Coach Schultz said.

"Let me," Jessica begged. She had forgotten all about her desire to go to Lovett Academy, now that she had seen the way they chose to compete. All she wanted was a chance to get even.

Todd was still sitting with Elizabeth. "Someone should take my place, too," he said in a low voice. "I don't think I want to be part of this anymore."

A hush fell over the crowd as everyone stared at Todd. Was it possible he was dropping out of the battle?

But there was no tearing Todd away from Elizabeth's side. Eventually a boy named Brent Calder volunteered to fill in for Todd, and the tug-of-war got under way. Courtney gave Todd a venomous look as everyone lined up to begin the final contest.

"OK," the Lovett coach said, helping the

students line up on either side of a chalk mark on the grassy field, "the first person on the other team must be pulled past this line for it to be a victory. Is that clear?"

"This isn't fair. We won, and they shouldn't get another chance," Courtney complained bitterly, her hands on her hips.

Jessica couldn't stand it anymore. "Shut up," she hissed to Courtney, who was standing near-by. "Or explain to your father how your team managed to win the College Bowl." The blistering look she gave Courtney made her fall back a few steps.

"I'll get you," she mouthed to Jessica. "Later."

Jessica just smiled. There was nothing Courtney could do to her, now that she wouldn't be attending Lovett. She would never even see her again! That thought made Jessica's pulse race with excitement, and she steadied her firm grip on the rope. "Ready...and...pull!" Coach Schultz yelled.

Wild cheers broke out as the tugging began. "Come on, Sweet Valley!" everyone screamed from one side of the field. "Come on, Lovett!" came from the other side.

Elizabeth's head was throbbing a little, but otherwise she was all right as she pressed closer to the front of the crowd with Todd. He kept one arm tightly around her waist.

At first Sweet Valley appeared to have the edge, then Lovett. Sweet Valley pulled back harder. "Come on! Pull!" Ken groaned, leaning back with all his might. Jessica's eyes were squeezed shut with the effort. "Pull! Pull!" Jeffrey yelled.

Jessica was at the front of the line, and she was getting yanked closer and closer to the chalk mark. Elizabeth could see that she was trying as hard as she could. Jessica's face was red from the intense effort, and a trickle of sweat ran down the side of her face.

That was when Todd stood up and screamed, "GO, SWEET VALLEY HIGH!"

Elizabeth felt her heart soar. Todd's cry seemed to fill the Sweet Valley High team with that extra bit of energy they needed. And, pulling together with all their might, they yanked the Lovett team over the mark. Sweet Valley High had won the tug-of-war—and the Battle of the Schools!

"Daddy, it isn't fair," Courtney complained. "You know we should have won. That rotten tug-of-war wasn't even planned."

"Courtney," her father said sternly, "I want

you to try very hard to be a good sport. The judges have decided that Sweet Valley High is the winner."

Courtney could barely look at him, or the spot where the other judges were presenting the Sweet Valley High students with a shining trophy. She pushed her way angrily through the crowd, her eyes darkening when she saw Jessica Wakefield.

"You cheat," she snapped. "If your sister had been on the tug-of-war team like she should have been, you never would have won."

"Don't talk to *me* about cheating," Jessica retorted. "I saw what you and your friend were doing with that curtain at the College Bowl."

The color drained from Courtney's face. "Don't you dare come to Lovett next year, or I'll make you good and sorry," she threatened. "Lila told me you were applying. And you know what? I can guarantee you right now you won't get in!"

Jessica gave her an imperious glare. "Who wants to go to your school, anyway?" She grinned. "I prefer to be with the *winning* team!" And with that she stalked off, leaving a furious Courtney staring after her.

Meanwhile, Todd was helping Elizabeth through the crowd, his arm still wrapped tightly around her.

"Thanks for helping out your team, Todd," Courtney said sarcastically as they passed by.

Todd stared at her. "I *was* helping my team," he said quietly. Then he turned back to Elizabeth. "Liz, if my parents agree to it, and if the school will allow it, I want to come back to Sweet Valley High," he said.

Courtney couldn't believe her ears. Todd really didn't know anything! "I hope you're very happy there," she sneered.

"I'm sure I will be!" Todd said, grinning at Elizabeth. Courtney thought she was going to be sick.

"Well, I guess now that you're transferring to Lovett, you won't be able to be in the lottery for the Kidd shoe commercials," Lila said smugly. A group had gathered at the Dairi Burger after the battle to celebrate their victory. Lila, Amy, and Jessica were sitting in a corner booth, drinking sodas and splitting an order of french fries.

"Oh, I don't know if I want to transfer to Lovett anymore," Jessica said nonchalantly.

"Why not?" Amy demanded. "I don't suppose it has anything to do with wanting to be on a winning team, does it?"

Jessica shrugged. "I have my reasons," she said, taking a french fry.

"You are so unfair, Jessica Wakefield," Amy said. "You only want to stick around now because we won. And now you want to horn in on the winning prize. I can't even believe you!"

Lila looked at Jessica with interest. "You really don't want to tell us why you changed your mind? It can't just be the chance of getting to be on the commercial."

"Maybe she got sick of sitting around studying for the exams," Amy said.

Jessica shook her head. "I just decided I don't like the people that go there, that's all," she said calmly. She didn't feel like telling anyone what she had seen Courtney Kane do that morning in the College Bowl. The fact was, Jessica wouldn't have put it past Courtney to have had something to do with the frayed rope that had caused Elizabeth's fall. She certainly didn't want to go to school with people like that.

Still, there was no point trying to explain it all to Lila and Amy. Jessica would have to admit that she had made a mistake, something she hated to do.

For once, though, Jessica didn't mind. She was so glad she wouldn't have anything more to do with Lovett that she couldn't care less what anyone thought. All that really mattered was that Elizabeth was not hurt and that Sweet Valley High had won the competition fair and square, with a little extra help from Todd!

That night Elizabeth and Todd couldn't take their eyes off each other. "Every time I think of what almost happened to you today, when I saw you there, lying so helplessly on the ground..." Todd said, a catch in his throat.

"I'm just glad it's all worked out so well," Elizabeth said tenderly as they walked hand in hand toward the Dairi Burger. "And I'm so glad you and your parents have straightened everything out about school." After a long, heartfelt talk, Todd and his parents had decided that Sweet Valley High was the best place for him to be. Elizabeth was overjoyed. She could barely believe that, Monday morning, Todd would be back at Sweet Valley High. It felt like the world had been set right again.

"You want to go in first, or should I?" Elizabeth said with a smile when they reached the front door.

Todd laughed. "You," he said.

Elizabeth opened the door. No sooner had she walked into the restaurant than thunderous applause burst out. When Todd came in, the applause and cheers became almost deafening. "Yea, Todd and Liz!"

For Elizabeth there were two moments that made the victory especially wonderful. The first was the warm embrace from her twin. And the second was the moment when Jeffrey came up to shake Todd's hand and to give Elizabeth a hug. That was when she really and truly knew that everything was going to be all right.

More than all right. It was going to be wonderful.

"Hey, what's going on with you and Ken?" Jessica asked Amy later when she came back to the table to get her jacket. The two had been almost inseparable all evening.

Amy shrugged. "I told you. I think he's really cute," she said. "We have a lot in common, too. See you later!" she called over her shoulder. Then she headed to the door, where Ken was waiting for her.

Jessica couldn't believe it. Amy Sutton—and Ken Matthews? They didn't strike her as a likely couple. Ken was such a good, regular, solid guy, and Amy was one of the most flirtatious, boy-crazy girls in the whole school. Still, stranger things had happened before.

Jessica wondered if Amy's sudden interest in

Ken had anything to do with the fact that it was the height of the football season, and with Ken as the captain of the team, Amy would get a lot of extra attention in the next few weeks as his girlfriend.

Of course, it was probably just that Ken was one of the best-looking guys at school. Jessica couldn't deny that. She had gone out with Ken a few times in the past herself.

But what worried Jessica was that Ken was the kind of guy who took things seriously. He would probably think Amy had more in mind than just fun.

It's strange for me to be thinking this, Jessica said to herself, *but I sure hope Amy doesn't break Ken's heart!*

Are Amy and Ken an item? Find out in Sweet Valley High #60, THAT FATAL NIGHT.

NOW

SWEET VALLEY HIGH®

IS A GAME!

- • RACE THROUGH THE HALLS OF SWEET VALLEY HIGH
- • MEET SWEET VALLEY'S MOST POPULAR GUYS
- • GO ON 4 SUPER DREAM DATES

You and your friends are students at Sweet Valley High! You can be Jessica, Elizabeth, Lila or Enid and go on a dream date. Live the excitement of the Junior Prom, or go to a Sweet Sixteen Party. You can go surfing or join the bike tour. Whatever you choose, be sure to watch out for the other girls. To keep you from winning, they might even steal your boyfriend.

YOU'LL FIND THIS
GREAT MILTON BRADLEY GAME
AT TOY STORES AND BOOK STORES
NEAR YOU!

☐	27416 SLAM BOOK FEVER #48	$2.95
☐	27477 PLAYING FOR KEEPS #49	$2.95
☐	27596 OUT OF REACH #50	$2.95
☐	27650 AGAINST THE ODDS #51	$2.95
☐	27720 WHITE LIES #52	$2.95
☐	27771 SECOND CHANCE #53	$2.95
☐	27856 TWO BOY WEEKEND #54	$2.95
☐	27915 PERFECT SHOT #55	$2.95
☐	27970 LOST AT SEA #56	$2.95
☐	28079 TEACHER CRUSH #57	$2.95
☐	28156 BROKEN HEARTED #58	$2.95
☐	28193 IN LOVE AGAIN #59	$2.95

<u>Prices and availability subject to change without notice</u>

Buy them at your local bookstore or use this page to order.
- -

Bantam Books, Dept. SVH7, 414 East Golf Road, Des Plaines, IL 60016

Please send me the books I have checked above. I am enclosing $_____
(please add $2.00 to cover postage and handling). Send check or money
order—no cash or C.O.D.s please.

Mr/Ms _____

Address _____

City/State _____ Zip _____

SVH7—10/89

Please allow four to six weeks for delivery.

EXCITING NEWS FOR ROMANCE READERS

Loveletters—the all new, hot-off-the-press Romance Newsletter. Now you can be the first to know:

What's Coming Up:
* Exciting offers
* New romance series on the way

What's Going Down:
* The latest gossip about the SWEET VALLEY HIGH gang
* Who's in love . . . and who's not
* What Loveletters fans are saying.

What's New:
* Be on the inside track for upcoming titles

If you don't already receive Loveletters, fill out this coupon, mail it in, and you will receive Loveletters several times a year. Loveletters . . . you're going to love it!

Please send me my free copy of **Loveletters**

Name _____ Date of Birth _____

Address _____

City _____ State _____ Zip _____

To: LOVELETTERS
    BANTAM BOOKS
    PO BOX 1005
    SOUTH HOLLAND, IL 60473

MURDER AND MYSTERY STRIKES

America's favorite teen series
has a hot new line
of
Super Thrillers!

It's super excitement, super suspense, and super thrills as Jessica and Elizabeth Wakefield put on their detective caps in the new SWEET VALLEY HIGH SUPER THRILLERS! Follow these two sleuths as they witness a murder ... find themselves running from the mob ... and uncover the dark secrets of a mysterious woman. SWEET VALLEY HIGH SUPER THRILLERS are guaranteed to keep you on the edge of your seat!

YOU'LL WANT TO READ THEM ALL!